Valley of the Giant

Tad Hardy

ChariotVICTOR
PUBLISHING
A DIVISION OF COOK COMMUNICATIONS

Join Rachel and Elliot on all their Truthquest adventures!

The Mountain That Burns Within
Valley of the Giant
Treasure of the Hidden Tomb

Chariot Books is an imprint of ChariotVictor Publishing
Cook Communications, Colorado Springs, CO 80918
Cook Communications, Paris, Ontario
Kingsway Communications, Eastbourne, England

VALLEY OF THE GIANT
© 1997 by Tad Hardy

All rights reserved. Except for brief excerpts for review purposes, no part of this book may be reproduced or used in any form without written permission from the publisher.

All Scripture quotations in this publication are from the *Holy Bible, New International Version*. Copyright ©1973, 1978, 1984, International Bible Society. Used by permission of Zondervan Publishing House. All rights reserved.

ISBN 0-7814-3002X
Designed by Andrea Boven
Cover illustration by John Lytle
Map illustration by Guy Wolek
First printing, 1997
Printed in the United States of America
01 00 99 98 97   5 4 3 2 1

*For Elliot's real cousins (so far) —
Dylan, Devon, Kristin, and Marc*

▲   ▲   ▲   ▲   ▲

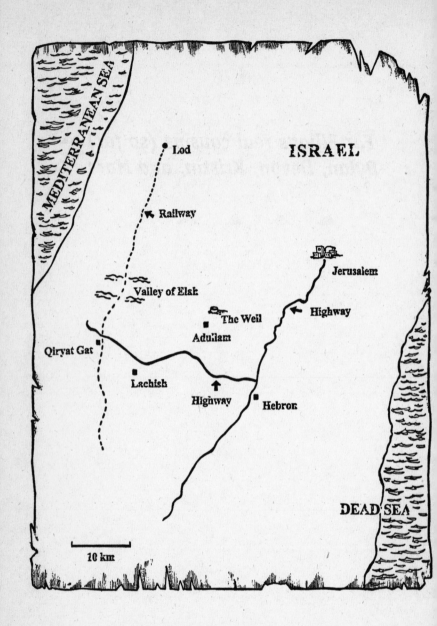

Places and Things in Israel

Adullam (uh-DULL-am) an archeological site southwest of Jerusalem

cister (SIS-turn) a chamber which collects rainwater

Elah (EE-lah) a valley west of Jerusalem

kibbutz (kib-UTS) a Jewish communal farm or settlement

Kidron (KID-rawn) a valley east of Jerusalem through which a brook flows

Lachish (LAY-kish) the archeological ruins of an ancient city with fortified walls

moshav (mow-SHAHV) a cooperative village made up of individual farms

ostraca (OSS-trak-ah) pieces of mudbrick or pottery containing ancient Hebrew writings

Philistines (FILL-eh-steen) "People of the Sea" who lived along the coastal plain of ancient Israel

Quiryat Gat (KIR-yat gat) a city in southwestern Israel

Selah (SEE-leh) a Hebrew musical tern of uncertain meaning

yoreh (YOR-eh) early rains signalling the beginning of the rainy season

CHAPTER 1

"Mother? Hello? Hello, Mother? Mother?" No reply. All Rachel heard was the silence of a dead telephone line and the hollow echo of her own British accent ringing in her ears. She punched the "talk" button on the cordless phone several times. "Mother, are you there?" Nothing. "Oh, rot!" She finally slammed the phone into the flattened pillow of her bottom bunk. A tiny cloud of dust puffed into the air and settled slowly back onto her rough blanket. "Of course you're not there. You weren't there when that ice storm closed the school last January and I had to walk two miles in freezing rain. Some teleconference with India, wasn't it? And you weren't around for the spring vocal concert either, when Harold Cooper fainted dead away off the back riser during the Mary Poppins medley." Rachel continued through her mental checklist and announced each item aloud as if her mother were there to hear. "Oh yes, and you didn't show for the nine-week parent-teacher conference last month. Every other fifth-grade parent managed to make it. That was your California trip, as I recall." She felt her lips tighten. "Why should I think you would be there now?"

"Because she lives there, that's why," answered the voice behind her.

Rachel turned slowly to find her cousin Elliot standing at the foot of the bunk bed.

"How long have you been lurking there?" Rachel demanded.

"Oh, you know me. I'm always here," Elliot replied.

"Please . . . don't remind me," she countered. She stood to look him squarely in the eyes, staring right through the dusty lenses of his wire-rimmed glasses. Her shadow, cast across Elliot's face by the morning sun glaring through the open window behind her, made her seem bigger and taller than him . . . another half inch and she *would* be. It wasn't fair that he got to be one week older and one-half inch taller. It just wasn't fair.

"It's rude to listen in on someone else's conversation," Rachel reminded him.

"I wouldn't call 'Oh, rot!' a conversation."

"You eavesdropped the entire time! Didn't anyone ever teach you manners and etiquette?" She could almost feel the steam rising from the top of her skull.

Elliot's brow wrinkled in mock thought beneath the brim of his dingy dig-site hat, the hat he wore practically everywhere, even to bed.

"Etiquette. I've heard that word before. I know! It's a vocabulary word, isn't it?" The smile that followed wasn't enough to disarm Rachel's ire.

"Right. As if," she huffed. As if Elliot wouldn't recognize a vocabulary word. He knew enough words to fill ten vocabulary books . . . something else that wasn't fair.

"So, I assume Aunt Lilia wasn't home?" For all of his occasional teasing, Elliot did have a knack for knowing when Rachel truly felt upset. He sat on the edge of the bunk, ready to listen. Rachel sat again and fumbled with the phone for a long moment before she spoke.

"Someone picked up. Someone answered, then suddenly the line went dead."

"Could be the phones," Elliot shrugged. "This isn't exactly a friends-and-family type calling location, you know." He slapped his hand against the bunk bed, creating another tiny dust cloud. "Or the phone batteries could be low, or . . ."

"You know what I think?" Rachel said, more to herself than to Elliot. "I think she hung up on me. I call her, from a thousand miles away . . ."

"More like six thousand miles, actually," he corrected her.

"Whatever. I call to tell her I'm fine and she clicks me off."

"Well, let's see . . ." Elliot stretched out his arm to reveal his space-age watch, complete with compass, stopwatch, alarm, and calculator. For all Rachel knew, he had a CD player and a refrigerator/freezer hidden in there as well. "It's 10 A.M. here in Israel, the sun's up, the birds are singing. And in Kentucky, eight time zones behind us . . ." He squinted his green eyes. "I'd say your mom just hung up on what sounded like a prank call. At two o'clock in the morning."

"She could have said hello," Rachel whispered under her breath.

"She probably never even woke up," Elliot went on, seeming to read her mind more than her lips. "Aunt Lilia is a pretty sound sleeper, isn't she?"

"The soundest." Rachel hid a weak smile as she remembered the times she had sneaked out after her mother had gone to sleep to play hide-and-go-seek in the dark with her best friend next door. But that was back in Kentucky and was not something Elliot needed to know. He knew enough already.

"What about Uncle Mason?" Rachel inquired. "Does he sleep soundly?"

"Same as Aunt Lilia. Which makes sense since they are brother and sister. Dad can sleep anywhere, anytime. When you spend half your life on cots and sleeping bags, you learn to sleep anywhere." Elliot repositioned his hat. "I'm learning, too, every time Dad takes me to another dig site."

"Well I'm not," Rachel informed him. "And I don't intend to learn the secret of sleeping in a drafty old building like this one, in the middle of nowhere, which is better suited to mice than to people. My bed in Kentucky does quite well, thank you." She studied the bunk bed. "In fact, I wish I were in it right now."

"You'd give up all of this excitement and discovery for one night's sleep?"

"You're not serious, are you?" she sneered. "I'd give up this sort of excitement for back-row tickets to a Ping-Pong match."

Elliot, obviously disgusted, rose in silence from the

bunk and nearly dropped the small, leather-bound book he had tucked under his arm. Immediately, Rachel felt her curiosity meter jump fifteen points.

"What's that?" she said abruptly, pointing to the book.

"What's what?" Elliot replied, half hiding the bound volume with his elbow. Rachel stared him down. "You mean this?" he said at last, tapping the book with his fingers.

"No, I mean that floppy thing at the end of your arm with five stumpy fingers hanging from it! Of *course* I mean that book, silly. What is it?"

"Uh . . . it's my journal. Sort of a record book." Elliot paused for a moment, then spilled his guts, just like Rachel knew he would. She had a knack for reading Elliot and his moods which, for the most part, were as predictable as clockwork. That knack often took advantage of Elliot's honesty. Honesty was one weakness Rachel managed to avoid. Like the plague.

"I keep a journal at each archeological site Dad and I visit," Elliot explained, "and I write down anything interesting—background information, new artifact finds, maps—you know, that kind of stuff."

"Oh." Rachel feigned boredom. She walked past him away from the window. Then she added casually over her shoulder, "I don't suppose you record things in there about nosy cousins."

Elliot answered just the way Rachel expected.

"No journal would be thick enough to hold all of that information."

"Then . . . you won't mind if I read it?" Rachel

dropped the first paw in her little game of mental cat-and-mouse.

"Well, there are a few personal observations in here, mainly scientific," he hedged.

"Sounds like a diary to me," Rachel said in the haughtiest voice possible.

"It isn't a diary, Rachel. Archeologists don't keep diaries. We keep journals."

"Oh, call it what you wish. It doesn't matter, really. I've already read in it." She hadn't, of course, but Elliot didn't know that. She decided to take a stab in the dark. "Like the part where you describe finding that inked pot, or whatever it is, made by the Flintstones."

"You mean the Philistine pottery?" came his hesitant reply.

"Right. The Frankenstein pots. I believe that's where you wrote, ' . . . Rachel keeps getting in the way. I'm surprised she hasn't broken something. I plan to spit in her hair while she's sleeping.'"

"I write that on every page," he laughed. Rachel didn't find his reply the least bit amusing, mainly because he had ended her hopes of getting a peek into the journal. For now. "I did record something you might find interesting, though. It involves the Englishman who established the dig site here at Lachish." Elliot popped the leather thong holding the journal's crinkled pages together. The pages opened like a Chinese fan.

"I've done a little research on the ruins here at Lachish and several other sites nearby. Some of the personal stories behind these digs in Israel are incredible."

Rachel pretended to cover a yawn.

"You're beginning to sound like a social studies exam. And I hate social studies, you know." She didn't let on, but the part about the Englishman caught her interest. After all, she had spent her first nine years in Great Britain before she and her mother moved to Kentucky two years ago. There wasn't a decent cup of tea in the entire state, but the weather in Kentucky sure beat England's. However, Kentucky's border rubbed right up against Indiana, where Elliot and Uncle Mason lived, which meant Rachel's mother could farm her out to them anytime she pleased. Which was most of the time.

"Dad's library back at the SIMA museum in Indiana has lots of background facts on ancient sites," he went on. "The Lachish dig opened up in the 1930s under British oversight. There must be half a dozen city walls stacked up here—maybe more." He stared wistfully out the window of the old barracks building at layers of limestone piled one on top of the other, representing a series of ancient cities that once stood on the site. "Anyway, this Englishman left the dig one day for a trip into town—"

"Probably looking for a decent cup of tea," Rachel jumped in.

"Maybe. But he never found it. Bandits bushwhacked him along a deserted road. He didn't survive." Elliot shook his head. "Hard to believe anyone could do such a thing, especially to an archeologist just doing his job."

"You know, I think my mother knew his family," Rachel lied.

"Really?" Elliot said, his eyes growing larger.

"I believe so. Yes! Now I remember! Mother said they told her the truth about what happened. The story going 'round said bandits, but actually he died from a disease common to many archeologists."

From the look on Elliot's face, Rachel guessed he hadn't come across this information in his readings.

"What disease?"

"Boredom." Rachel flipped her hair in smug satisfaction.

Elliot closed his journal and snapped the cover shut with an angry twist of his wrist.

"You shouldn't make light of something so awful. I just thought you might like to know a little history about the dig."

"No, you just thought that little story of yours would frighten me, make me hunker down in the corner of these drafty barracks and whine myself to sleep each night."

Elliot quickly regained his smile.

"You don't usually need an excuse to whine. I just wanted you to be aware of—"

"I know what you wanted," she retorted, cutting him off. "I know what you wanted, and it isn't going to work. This place is nothing more than a pile of chalk rock that's older than dirt. Your stories don't change that. I don't scare easily, you know."

The words had scarcely left Rachel's lips when a deafening *whack* ricocheted from the outside wall of the barracks. With a *zing*, something small and fast flew just above her head through the open window.

Moments later, she found herself cowering against the legs of the bunk bed, holding tightly to the scratchy blanket thrown across it.

"They're firing on us!" she cried aloud. "Someone's taking the dig by force! Take cover!"

Elliot, unfazed, walked across the room to the foot of the bunk. He squatted, lifted a small stony fragment from the floor, and held it before one eye.

"What . . . what is it?" Rachel stuttered. She expected to hear a lecture on bullets and handguns.

After a long, dramatic pause, Elliot turned to her and answered. "Chalk rock."

Rachel flew to her feet and craned her neck through the open window, fire sizzling at her eyelids.

"All right! Who threw that rock?" she bellowed with the mustered courage of a lion.

A local dig worker carving out a hollow near one ancient city wall nodded and waved sheepishly.

"My apologies," came his quiet reply. "This stone split as I broke out the soil with my pickax."

Rachel grabbed the length of her hair in her fist and shook it in his direction. "What do I look like? Target practice? I could have a concussion right now! You're lucky my forehead isn't split like a melon! You almost—"

Elliot gently but firmly moved her from the window and leaned out himself. He returned the worker's bashful wave.

"No harm done," he called out.

Rachel glared.

"He's crazy. *You're* crazy. Uncle Mason should fire him."

"Doesn't work that way. All I know is, we're lucky—"

"Lucky?" Rachel butted in. "I should say so. I could have been killed, just like that Englishman."

Elliot smiled.

"All I know is," he repeated, "we're lucky . . . you don't scare easily."

CHAPTER 2

The flying rock episode was still fresh in Rachel's mind when Uncle Mason entered the barracks—so much so that her hands still had a case of the jitters, thanks to Elliot, Mr. Dig-Site Dweeb.

Mason Conner, a big yet gentle man, breezed through the doorway carrying several shards of pottery. He had hardly broken a sweat in the fresh November air. He was an outgoing sort, good with people, and had an easy way about him, except for his ceaseless curiosity and the intensity in his eyes. In that way, Elliot and his father were very much alike.

Without a word, he pinched a pair of narrow spectacles onto the bridge of his nose as he strode past them, walking between the cots lining either side of the barracks building and into the separate kitchen area, which sometimes doubled as a dig site workroom. He then divided the handful of shard fragments into three neat piles on the cabinet top near the sink. He plucked the proper cleaning brush from among those stored along the wall in old coffee cans. Then he selected a small eyedropper bottle of liquid from the shelf and set to work cleaning the shards as if each piece were made of fine china.

"What did you find, Dad?" Elliot asked.

"Ostraca." Uncle Mason's intent stare remained fixed on the pottery.

"Wow!" came Elliot's excited reply. "Pre- or post-Assyrian?"

"Mmm . . . good question."

"Question?" Rachel spouted. "That was a question? It sounded more like a sneeze!" Between the flying rocks and the boring archeological mumbo jumbo, Rachel had had quite enough. "Would someone mind ever so much telling me what is going on here? First I'm bombarded by shooting stones, and now I'm stuck in a drafty bunkhouse with two men . . ." she looked at Elliot, "well, one man and one rodent in a hat and glasses . . . " She caught her breath, suddenly realizing that both Elliot and Uncle Mason wore a hat and glasses. Before Elliot could seize on her mistake, she quickly turned toward the wall and pretended to address a large audience. " . . . both of whom have gone gaga over fistfuls of shattered flowerpots. And now," she called out, "they think they've found a fossilized ostrich."

"Not an ostrich," Elliot said cheerfully. "An ostracon—one of those Frankenstein pots you're so interested in."

Uncle Mason finally looked away from the pot fragments for a moment.

"Goodness Agnes!" he chuckled. "What are you two talking about?"

"Nothing, actually," Rachel answered first. "Elliot and I were just discussing the scientific merits of artifacts collected here at La-cheese."

"La-keesh," Elliot corrected her pronunciation. He adjusted his hat. "Rachel thinks the Flintstones lived here."

"Oh, that was just an archeologist joke," she defended. She stared daggers through Elliot. "Besides, I find it tiresome keeping up on all of the names you banter around—Philistines, Nectarines, and all that."

The wrinkle in Uncle Mason's brow deepened, and a quizzical look crossed his chipper face.

"Uhh . . . right. At any rate, it's best you both 'bone up' on your knowledge of the dig site—no pun intended. We'll be entertaining guests for dinner."

"Who's coming, Dad?"

"Ian Cunningham, an old and dear friend of mine. And he's bringing a colleague with him from the British Museum."

Rachel perked up.

"The British Museum? The one in London?"

"That's the one. Have you been there?" Uncle Mason asked.

"I seem to recall taking a field trip to some museum, back in primary school. I imagine it was the British Museum."

Elliot's jaw dropped in disbelief.

"You've been to the British Museum and you don't remember it?"

"Of course I remember it," she snapped. Actually she remembered very little about it. She wasn't even cer-

tain it *had* been the British Museum. All museums
looked alike to her—all two or three she had ever
bothered to enter. "It had the usual displays. Lots of
dusty old stuff—beads and cracked pots and bones
and that sort of thing—very much like SIMA, only
immensely larger." SIMA, the Southern Indiana
Museum of Archeology where Uncle Mason worked
and taught, had dusty old items. It seemed safe that
most other museums did, too.

"Did you see the Babylonian artifacts?" Elliot's
curiosity always caught up with her sooner or later.

Rachel threw up her arms with a dramatic flourish.

"Do I look like a walking museum exhibit? I don't
make a habit of memorizing every gold urn, clay pot,
and mummy face I've ever seen, whether it's Bubble-
gumian or otherwise."

"Mummies?" Elliot jumped in. "They let you see the
mummies?"

Uncle Mason cleared his throat loudly, getting their
full attention.

"As I was saying," he said with a smile, "Dr.
Cunningham and Dr. Chatsworth have a great deal of
work to do and precious little time to accomplish it. I'll
expect you both to be available to help them out as
best you can. *Together.*" He pushed the word "together"
from his mouth as though it were a threat.

"No problem," Elliot answered, looking at Rachel.

"Sounds jolly good to me," Rachel said, not returning
Elliot's glance.

Oh, what a lovely turn of events! she thought. Her
anger with herself at being frightened quickly drained

away. Two British archeologists soon would arrive and she would no longer be the only Brit at the dig. Elliot wouldn't dare tell another story about murdered Englishmen. He would be outnumbered! And the two men would bring tea, no doubt—what a delicious thought. Thanksgiving in Israel might not be so bad after all.

"They'll be here before dark," Uncle Mason continued, "probably traveling by Jeep with an Israeli government escort. They've spent the last two days in the hill country near Hebron. I plan to bunk them in the beds along the far wall. You two don't mind sharing the barracks with a couple of crusty old archeologists like myself, do you?"

"On the contrary," Rachel said sweetly. "I'm quite looking forward to visitors from the civilized world." She finally threw a deliberate stare in Elliot's direction.

"Magnificent," Uncle Mason boomed with his usual exuberance. He handed the pottery fragments to Elliot. "Enter these into the artifact log for me, would you, please?" Then he was off again in a blur of activity, headed back to the crumbled walls outside.

Rachel followed behind, anxious to get a breath of fresh air beyond the barracks. She settled against one of the outer walls, near where the gate to some forgotten city had towered centuries before, and stared at the surrounding hillsides. During their hour-long ride from Tel Aviv's coastal beaches to Lachish two days ago, Elliot, the Self-Appointed Tour Guidemaster, had remarked how the hills of Judea symbolized the true beauty of all Israel. On a blue-sky morning like this

one, Rachel almost had to believe him. From the
Lachish site, at least two oak groves and a vineyard
were visible. Distant oaks dotted the bone-brown soil
like so many broccoli sprouts and blended together
into a bumpy blanket of green spread over the rolling
hills beyond. The vineyard lay much closer, in a plot of
land set apart from terraced vegetable gardens by
limestone walls which resembled the cobblestone
streets in older parts of Britain. Occasionally, a small
stretch of land arose where bare blocks of chalk rock
caught the shadows of lone olive trees.

"Pretty nice view, isn't it?" Elliot observed as he came
to lean beside her. "You can tell why so many cities
were built here over the past three thousand years.
Everything is especially green right now since the
rains came early this fall. Lucky for us we hit a dry
spell . . . otherwise we'd be ankle deep in mud this
time of year." He tipped his hat brim and pointed due
east. "The Dead Sea sits on the other side of those
hills, and somewhere past that higher range," he continued, pointing north across newly planted crop fields,
"is Jerusalem."

Rachel noticed a pair of white tube-like buildings
standing near the crop fields.

"What are those?" she asked, hoping to stump him.
"They look like . . . ," she squinted. " . . . like hula-
hoops wearing long underwear."

Elliot laughed out loud.

"Almost. They're hothouses. The farmers probably
grow vegetable seedlings inside of them."

"Probably?" Rachel challenged. "You mean, you don't

know for sure? Oh, my, my, my . . . this is highly irregular. I'm shocked and deeply troubled."

"Funny, Rachel. Most of the machinery and farm buildings in this area are owned by the *moshav* in sort of a co-op type arrangement. The farmers simply share equipment costs to make more money on their crops. I like that idea."

"I'm certain you do," she agreed. After a calculated silence she added, "I know . . . why don't you plan to stay here for a while—like, maybe for the next hundred years or so. I'll return to the States with Uncle Mason while you share tractors and dig up clay ostriches." Israeli tractors and the farmers who shared them held little appeal for Rachel. This *moshav* guy, whoever he was, sounded a great deal more interesting. He must be in charge; otherwise, why would he own all of the big stuff?

Just as Uncle Mason had promised, a Jeep rolled into camp shortly after lunch, carrying two men and a driver. Rachel knew the older man was British simply by the way he hopped from the jeep—gracefully, with calm, complete control. His white cotton shirt fit his small frame neatly. He was trim and spry and walked briskly, an equipment bag strapped over one shoulder. After chatting with the Jeep driver briefly, he raised an arm of greeting in their direction. Uncle Mason strode over to meet him with a warm handshake.

They exchanged the usual pleasantries typical of such professional meetings, calling each other "doctor"

this and "doctor" that and looking quite reserved.
Finally, Uncle Mason's face broke into a limitless
smile.

"Ian, you old mountain goat, you!" he bellowed, clasp-
ing the older man's shoulders tightly with his out-
stretched palms. "It is good to see you again. How
long's it been, three years?"

Dr. Cunningham's playful eyes reflected Uncle
Mason's smile.

"Oh, no, Mason. Four years. The Turkish Conference,
wasn't it? You're getting a bit forgetful in your old age,
what?" Then his playful eyes fell upon Rachel and
Elliot. "And these? These must be your two exquisite
children. Why, you old fossil, you never told me of a
lovely daughter. You've been hiding her from me,
haven't you?"

"Dr. Ian Cunningham, meet my son, Elliot." Elliot
nodded dutifully and shook the professor's hand. "And
this," Uncle Mason went on, "is my niece, Rachel
Ashton."

"How do you do?" Rachel said politely.

"You're a Brit," he observed. "How delightful!"

"I was, actually. I live in Kentucky now, with my
mother."

"Ahh, yes. But you were born in Britain. Not far from
London, would be my guess. I hear it in your voice."
He winked, but his smooth complexion barely showed
a wrinkle. "Enjoy a spot of tea now and again, do you?"

Rachel felt herself relax for the first time since they
had arrived in Israel. She knew how it felt to be alone
in a strange land. Leaving England and spending the

last two years in Kentucky had been difficult at times. Coming to Israel, even for a week-long archeological expedition, brought back some of those uneasy feelings. Dr. Cunningham made her feel at home again.

The second archeologist stepped forward. "Nigel Chatsworth," he said, shaking first Elliot's hand, then her own. "You can call me Nigel."

"Oh, yes." Dr. Cunningham rubbed his brow in embarrassment. "Of course . . . this is Dr. Chatsworth, a colleague from the Museum. So sorry, Nigel."

Nigel forced a smile. He was a young-looking man, nearly as tall as Uncle Mason, but of slighter build. Indeed, looking at him was almost like looking at Elliot twenty years into the future—the same toothy grin, dressed hat to toe in pressed khakis, eager to stand in the sun all day long staring at piles of old rocks. After a moment or two of awkward silence, Nigel spoke again.

"I believe I shall get our bags." He returned to the Jeep, slung several luggage straps over his shoulders, and disappeared into the barracks doorway as Dr. Cunningham watched.

"Nigel's specialty is Bronze Age cultures and artifacts," he informed Uncle Mason. "He's quite good."

"I'm sure he is, Ian. You rarely bother with anything but the best."

"Well, now," Dr. Cunningham shifted gears, "let's have a look at the famous walls of Lachish, shall we then?"

Their conversation quickly faded into chalk-rock talk. Elliot tagged along behind the two old friends, while Rachel politely excused herself to make a beeline for the barracks. First things first. Had they remembered the tea?

Inside, she found Nigel standing at the foot of a bunk bed, sorting through his travel bag on the top bunk.

"So, Dr. Chatsworth . . . I mean, Nigel, how was your trip?" she asked, trying to show great interest.

"Quite good, thank you." He seemed preoccupied with unzipping compartments on the bag, moving items from one compartment to another, and rezipping them. Rachel tried to wait patiently, but the anticipation nearly killed her. "There!" he finally said. "Just had to get a few things rummaged through. Setting up camp and all, you know." Quickly he stuffed the travel bag behind the bunk, separate from the remaining luggage. A long, weary sigh followed, after which he hung his hat on the bedpost. "Now . . . let's have a cup of tea, shall we? Have you a clean pot?"

Rachel felt herself smile. This Thanksgiving expedition was beginning to shape up quite nicely. Quite nicely indeed.

CHAPTER 3

"That's a nasty scar Nigel has on his wrist . . . did you notice it?" Rachel handed Elliot another raw egg, which he cracked open over the small kitchen sink. Uncle Mason had served a local dish to their British guests for dinner last night. Now it was Elliot and Rachel's turn in the kitchen, making breakfast—a chore Rachel tried to avoid, but couldn't.

"No, but I don't make a habit of examining other people's wrists," Elliot replied slowly.

"Obviously you don't bother to look at your own, either, or you would have seen that egg yolk smeared all over your shirtsleeve."

"Where?" He jolted, nearly dropping the egg in his rush to gawk at his forearms. Rachel immediately burst into laughter. There was nothing there, of course. Elliot shook his head in disgust, and his sandy hair flopped side to side as he did so. Rachel had persuaded him to cook without the benefit of his smelly old hat. That way, she didn't have to look at it.

"But really," Rachel plowed on, between more laughs

at Elliot's expense, "it's quite odd."

"What's odd?"

"The scar . . . on Nigel's wrist!"

"Oh, yeah. I'd forgotten what you were talking about," he mumbled. "I usually don't pay much attention." He tumbled the egg into a worn iron skillet.

"Ughhh!" Rachel hated it when Elliot had the last word. She grabbed the carton of eggs away from him. "I can do this! Why don't you go do something useful. Like drown."

He leaned against the sink and crossed his arms. "So . . . tell me about Dr. Chatsworth's wrist."

Normally Rachel would have refused to tell him anything, but she couldn't stop thinking about her afternoon with Nigel Chatsworth.

"Well, we made a pot of tea yesterday, shortly after he and Dr. Cunningham arrived. And while we were chatting, I noticed an ugly scar on his left wrist."

"Did he tell you how he got it?"

"Of course not! You don't think I asked him, do you?"

Elliot shrugged. "Sometimes the only way to get answers is to ask questions."

"Only for someone rude like you." Elliot wasn't really rude. In fact, most people fawned over him and told Uncle Mason how grown-up he seemed. But Rachel saw it as her mission to keep him humble. It was a mission she enjoyed thoroughly.

Elliot tilted his hatless head to one side. "So you plan to rely on your usual refined method of collecting information: snoop until you find out for yourself."

"Precisely."

Elliot pulled another egg from the carton.

"Did you know Dr. Chatsworth is driving the supply truck over to Qiryat Gat after breakfast?" he asked.

"To where? Cat Gut? Where on earth is that? It sounds disgusting!"

"No, Qiryat Gat. It's a city about ten kilometers west of here. Closest place to pick up supplies. Anyway, he's headed over there, and he's invited us to ride along. Dad says it's okay."

"Finally!" Rachel huffed. "A chance to see something besides bunk beds and eggs. I'm sure Nigel enjoyed my company yesterday and is anxious for us to spend more time together. He probably asked you along just to be polite." She waited for Elliot's reply, but it never came. "And I do think you should call him Nigel," she added.

"'Dr. Chatsworth' is fine with me."

"Why? He asked us to call him . . . wait a minute—you're jealous, aren't you?" she accused.

"What are you talking about?" Elliot said, turning to face her and giving away his true feelings in the process.

"You're jealous. Of Nigel."

"That's crazy."

"No, it isn't. It makes perfect sense. From what he said at dinner last night, he has traveled all over the world and made important discoveries. He and Uncle Mason are quite chummy already. And he appears to be wealthy as well, for a man who is only thirty years old. So Mr. Junior Archeologist here is jealous."

Immediately Rachel sensed she had struck a sore spot

and considered offering an apology. But she didn't.

"On the contrary." Elliot thrust out his chest. "I'm looking forward to learning a lot from him. He's a very detailed and precise scientist. He's very careful."

"Unlike you with your eggs." Rachel pointed to the cookstove where half a dozen forgotten eggs smoldered in the skillet like brown lava.

As usual, Elliot's apparent disappointment with himself over the burned omelette hid any anger he might have felt for Rachel. After all, she had deliberately distracted him long enough to ruin everything. But he didn't scream or holler or throw silverware like she would have done. He didn't blame her for letting breakfast burn. Instead, he simply said, "I'll get another skillet. Crack some more eggs, okay?"

"Right!" she called after him. "Go on then, pretend you're not angry with me! Later you'll write something absolutely horrid about me in that diary of yours, won't you? Won't you!"

No reply. She heard only the clatter of pots and pans from the walk-in pantry. A minute later he emerged from the pantry with a skillet and a smile.

"What on earth are you smiling about?" Rachel scowled. "You just burned enough eggs to kill all the chickens in Israel."

"Look what I found." He held a clean skillet under his arm and a blunt metal object, black and rusted with age, in his hand.

"What is it?"

Elliot's free hand dove into his pants pocket and pulled out a small shiny rectangle. He held it several inches above the object, then dropped it. The magnet clamped tightly to the black chunk in his hand with a dull *clank*.

"It's iron," Elliot confirmed.

"Well, I can see that! So is that stupid skillet under your arm. Do you plan to burn eggs on everything in the pantry?"

"This," he said, shaking the dark hunk of metal, "is a spear point—an iron spear point common to this part of Israel."

"So what? Skillets are common here, too," Rachel huffed.

"Uh-huh. But not 3,000-year-old skillets." He searched the kitchen until he found his hat, then cinched it over his head as if locking on a thinking cap. "What would an ancient spear point be doing in the pantry?" he wondered aloud.

"The same thing you're doing . . . looking for clean cookware," Rachel retorted. "Frankly, I don't know and I don't care. Now, shall we finish making breakfast before these eggs turn into chickens?"

"I'd better show this to Dad and the others," Elliot said, ignoring her as he strode toward the door, the clean skillet still tucked under his elbow.

"Wait!" Rachel cried. "You can't just leave me here with all of this work! And bring back that skillet!"

Too late. Mr. Spear Head and his iron artifacts had slipped through the kitchen doorway.

"I hope that magnetic brain of yours attracts that spear right into your forehead!" she yelled after him.

"I say, pretty tough talk for a Brit, isn't it?"

Nigel Chatsworth's soothing accent caught her off guard.

"Oh!" Rachel's heart nearly jumped from her chest. "Nigel! You startled me. I didn't hear you come in."

"I suppose not, over all of that yelling and whatnot," he joked.

"With Elliot, you mean?" She made a quick recovery. "Pardon the expression, but he's such a peabrain sometimes. Here I am slaving away in the kitchen, and he walks away from all of this work."

Nigel gingerly lifted the carton of eggs from her hands.

"Here, let me give you a hand."

"That's very kind of you. Unlike *some* people!" she called out toward the kitchen door, just in case Elliot was within earshot. "I'm glad you happened by. I was afraid our late breakfast might delay our trip to Cat Guts."

"I take it you mean the supply trip, to Qiryat Gat?" Nigel chuckled. "The city isn't far—only a twenty-minute ride, actually. Although it's a bit of a bumpy jaunt, particularly in the supply truck. There is a train station there. I thought you and Elliot might enjoy a short hop on the train if you like. Getting supplies for a bunch of crusty dirt-diggers like myself isn't terribly glamorous." He emptied the egg carton. "Perhaps I'll do the shopping while you two take a quick northern run up the railway. How does that sound?"

"A passenger train?" Rachel perked up. "I haven't ridden since leaving Britain. How quaint. You meet such interesting people on the train, you know."

"The scenery through the valley south of Kidron is marvelous."

"I'd very much like to see something beyond these rock walls and ruins," she confided. "The train sounds lovely."

"It's a date then. The three of us shall leave after breakfast."

Finally! Something to look forward to besides cracked pots and crackpots. Rachel felt a twinge of excitement for the first time in days.

They worked together in silence for a time, Rachel scrambling eggs, and Nigel toasting bread slices from loaves baked the day before by an Israeli field assistant. He certainly seemed to know his way around the kitchen for never having been there before.

"So," Nigel finally said, "I believe I heard you mention a spear of some sort? Not something you plan to use on poor, unsuspecting Elliot, I trust."

Rachel smiled her best schoolgirl smile. "No, not yet, anyway. Elliot did say he found one here in the pantry, however."

"A spear? Seems an odd place to store old weaponry," he laughed.

"Elliot said the same thing."

"He's a bright one, that Elliot," Nigel said softly.

"For a peabrain," Rachel added, even more softly.

CHAPTER 4

"Look at this, Rachel," Elliot muttered, slowly tracing his finger along a narrow blue line in the travel guidebook on his lap. "It's the train route Dr. Chatsworth told us about at breakfast. He'll drop us off at the train station here," he said, tapping a spot on the map that read *Qiryat Gat*, "then we ride north toward the city of Lod and back again. Should take four hours or so."

"Where did you get that?" Rachel asked suspiciously.

"From Dr. Chatsworth . . . Nigel, I mean."

Rachel pressed both hands against the dashboard of the old supply truck and turned a practiced smile toward Elliot, seated next to her in the passenger seat.

"Oh! So it's Nigel now! Not three hours ago you refused to call him anything but Dr. Chatsworth. He gives you a travel guidebook and now you're on a first-name basis." She prepared to rub it in. Besides, she still hadn't evened the score with Elliot for skipping out on kitchen duty earlier, leaving her to cook breakfast alone . . . alone until Nigel came to her rescue.

Elliot shrugged. "Relax, Rachel. It was good of him to

help clear the breakfast dishes and . . ."

"*And* help *cook* breakfast as well, unlike some people," Rachel interrupted.

He grew silent for a moment, then looked back at her. "I thought about what you said . . . about my being jealous of Nigel. Maybe I was a little jealous. I just didn't realize it."

"I'll take that as an apology," she snapped back. "Although it's not a terribly good one, nor does it cover you for skipping out at breakfast."

"Right," he replied. "That spear point in the pantry sort of caught my attention, didn't it?"

Rachel didn't offer him the dignity of a response, choosing instead to give him the silent treatment as punishment. At least he had admitted he was wrong—something she could never be accused of doing. Why did Elliot always have to be so . . . so honest and sincere?

The driver's-side door of the supply truck suddenly flew open and in climbed Nigel.

"Shall we be off, then?" he said cheerily, removing his hat and handing it to Rachel for safekeeping. "That is, if old Bertha here will motor us over our little back road to Qiryat Gat." With a sharp slap to the dusty dashboard, he pumped the foot pedal hard with the heel of his leather boot three times, while bowing over the steering wheel as if whispering gently to the dented old truck. "Come on, old girl," he muttered aloud. The starter whirred several times before finally cranking over with a terrible clatter. Rachel, startled, pressed her fingers to her ears. Another loud clank shook the floor beneath her feet as Nigel threw the truck into gear and it lurched forward. The whine of the engine rose and fell with each turn of the bouncy tires carrying them away from the dig site toward Qiryat Gat.

When they reached the main road, which appeared to be little more than a wide scrape of bumpy dirt between two weedy patches of green, Nigel nodded toward Elliot.

"I see you're studying the train routes. Good idea."

"He would study a gum wrapper if you let him," Rachel butted in. Sitting between these two dirt-diggers all the way to Cat Gut was not a pleasant thought, especially if the two of them planned to compare notes on how to clean a pickax, or which dig-site hat styles were in fashion this season. She was prepared to nip that sort of talk in the bud before it began.

Elliot folded the guidebook neatly into the canvas satchel strapped across his shoulder—the silly Pony Express bag Rachel hated almost as much as she hated his ridiculous hat. In doing so, he had to remove several books packed inside, including his journal.

"Oh, marvelous," Rachel bounced out between dips and bumps in the road, "we're all about to be immortalized in Mr. Pony Express Bag's diary. Let me see . . . what should you write today? How about 'Rode to Cat Gut with two intelligent companions. Made me feel stupid.' "

Elliot said nothing, but he opened the leather thong holding the covers together and fingered through the pages slowly, holding them at just the right angle so she couldn't quite snoop. He did that on purpose, she was sure of it.

"Good idea, that. Keeping a journal, I mean," Nigel announced over the truck's noisy gears. "I keep one myself, actually."

"I'm sure yours is much more interesting than Elliot's," Rachel bluffed. Actually, she longed to flip through the pages of Elliot's journal for a peek into that intriguing brain of his. Particularly if the contents pertained to her.

"Nigel probably keeps the same kinds of notes I do." Elliot looked past Rachel and spoke directly to the dashing British archeologist beside her. "Landmarks, discoveries, bits of local information that might come in handy. Right?"

"Absolutely." He smiled an odd smile but said no more.

Rachel settled into the cracked upholstery of the supply truck's bench-type seat as best she could. She was outnumbered two to one. Worse yet, she was surrounded. So she decided to keep silent for a time, hoping Elliot would write in his precious diary, and Nigel would keep his eagle eyes on the ribbon of dirt he called a road.

As they drew closer to Cat Gut, the road widened and the bumps lessened. Now and again they met a local resident riding a bicycle, or passed a small house set back from the road. An occasional chicken or goat or cattle egret appeared at the road's edge. Rachel marveled at how different the people of the countryside appeared compared with the urban bustle of travelers at the Tel Aviv airport, where her first encounter with Israel began, four long days ago.

With each passing kilometer, the chalky hills of Judea shrank ever so slightly behind them. A patchwork of stony farm fields fit between green grassy pastures flecked with yellow wildflowers from the early fall rains. Soon the olive-tree-grays and grass-shoot-greens blended together into a backdrop for the soft browns and reds of the buildings in Cat Gut, straight ahead. Like a racecar driver, Nigel wheeled the old truck through several sharp curves in the road, and, crossing one final bump, squeaked into a small parking lot beside the railway station. It looked to Rachel like a cross between some small-town courthouse in Kentucky and a prison. The flat-topped building had two sets of arched windows mounted in a two-story structure of limestone blocks. A modest waiting area of dirt and stone stretched between the station doors and the train tracks. Nigel edged the truck onto a leveled drive near the railway station entrance.

"Well, here we are, then," he said in characteristic British fashion, ending his comment on a high, hopeful note. "Qiryat Gat railway station. Tour guide to all of Israel," he joked.

No sooner had he spoken than the train engine chugged into the station from the south, wheels clicking at a slowed pace against the rails. Elliot and Nigel both checked their watches.

"Right on time, according to the blue route schedule," Elliot confirmed.

"Was it really necessary to tell me that?" Rachel said. Nigel and Elliot both chuckled, and she found herself hoping that only one ticket remained for the trip to Lod and back. Elliot could walk, as far as she was concerned. Or crawl, perhaps.

The train engine and its four passenger cars looked more like a traveling circus than a passenger railway. Their bright red tops, brilliant blue sides, and paneless windows bore little resemblance to the commuter train cars Rachel remembered from merry old England. She almost expected an elephant or tiger to step from the train, instead of the handful of robed travelers that exited its doorways.

"Best you hurry in and get your tickets," Nigel said as he revved the old truck. Again, he checked his watch. "It's nearly ten o'clock. I'll be back by four at the latest. Have a jolly good time, won't you? You will see a beautiful part of Israel few visitors take time to enjoy."

Rachel handed him his hat and followed Elliot out the passenger door. With a final growl from the truck engine, Nigel left the station, headed across town for supplies. Elliot cinched his satchel against his shoulder.

"I'll run in here and pick up our tickets," he offered. He disappeared through the train station door. Immediately Rachel strode to the train, selected one of the five passenger cars, and peered into the open doorway. Inside lay a narrow aisle separating pairs of upholstered booths, almost like booths in a restaurant. Shafts of sunlight poured in through the open windows. Nearly half of the booths were filled, mainly by local travelers. She stepped to the next railcar, nearer the engine, where a mixture of locals and tourists filled most of the booths. This car looked interesting—but only a few booths remained unoccupied.

Rachel waited impatiently for Elliot's dingy hat and goofy bag to emerge from the station. When they did, she beckoned to him with a wide sweep of her arm. He ambled in her direction, calmly rubbing the tickets together between his fingers.

"This isn't the train to Snail Land!" she called out, waving him on. "Hurry up!"

"Here," he said, holding out a ticket when he reached the train.

"Now I know why it takes years of digging for archeologists to find one simple old clay pot—they're all as slow as you!" she fumed. "I hope you realize you've nearly cost us our seats." She stomped up the railcar steps ahead of Elliot and led him to an empty booth at the rear of the car.

"What's your rush?" he asked, once they were seated. "This is supposed to be a relaxing trip, remember? Sightseeing, learning . . ."

"Traveling with you is nearly as relaxing as a dip in a pool filled with piranhas."

Elliot shrugged and opened his Pony Express bag. Moments later, the train began to inch forward. The chalk-rock station faded slowly away behind them.

Rachel passed the next few minutes in silence, watching the outskirts of Cat Gut pass her window. With each turn of the train wheels the breeze on her face grew stronger. At last, the train entered the countryside, surrounded by sloping hills, flattened pastures,

small trees, and an occasional spot of terraced farm-
land, all beneath a clear blue sky. The lyrical rocking of
the wheels lulled her deeper into her seat. It also
brought back memories of train travel in Europe years
ago, when her mother would whisk her off to some
governess for a day or two while attending work meetings. She remembered how, as a little girl, she would
waltz up and down the railcar aisles, charming candy
away from all of the passengers with big smiles. Her
mother never seemed to appreciate those smiles quite
as much as her fellow travelers.

"Rachel," Elliot said, drawing his camera from the
satchel, "stand over there for a second. I'll get a picture
of you." He motioned her toward the aisle.

Rachel brushed him off.

"I know what I look like, thank you."

"Oh, come on. We'll send it to Aunt Lilia in
Kentucky."

"Are you insane?" she said through clenched teeth. "I
am not about to make a complete fool of myself in front
of all of these people. Especially not over a photo for
Mother."

"They're tourists. Goodness Agnes, *we're* tourists.
Tourists are supposed to take pictures. We're even
allowed to make fools of ourselves."

"Excuse me." Two teenage girls appeared at Rachel's
shoulder, and one addressed Elliot. "I also have the
camera," she said in halting English with a strong
French accent. "You will take pictures?" She pointed to
herself and her friend.

"Uh . . . sure." Elliot glanced at Rachel. "Be right

back." Laying his satchel aside, he stood, caught his balance in the moving train, then trailed the girls toward the rear of the car where more of the French-speaking teenagers and their cameras congregated.

Rachel set her jaw and stared at the carpet-green pasture and fluttering tree branches clicking past her open window like snapshots. So . . . Elliot wanted to flit around and take pictures with his new little friends? And ignore her? Fine. She could do the same thing. Surely there was someone she could befriend. Out of spite, mainly. She surveyed the booths nearby. Let's see . . . a dozen more teenage tourists having a splendid time together, a handful of bearded men, two children barely tall enough to rest their chins on the railcar windowsills, one lightly-bearded old woman across the aisle who appeared to dislike children in general, and two smartly-dressed Israeli businessmen.

She opted for the businessmen. She stood, glanced one last time out the window, then stepped around the padded seat into the railcar aisle. Instantly she realized she no longer remembered how to walk on a moving train. One knee buckled, and Rachel found herself tumbling helplessly toward the white head covering of the bearded old woman. She groped for something . . . anything . . . to stop her fall, and managed to graze a seatback with her arm. Still, she landed square in the center of the old woman's wide lap. The startled woman met Rachel's arrival with a gasp.

"Oh! I'm dreadfully sorry!" Rachel blurted out. "I didn't . . . the train just . . . my knees . . ." All she heard was the laughter of the passengers and the clacking of the wheels on the rails beneath her. Her worries of making a fool of herself were over now. She had done it, and done it well. All thanks to Elliot and his "Mr. Friendly" let-me-take-the-tourists'-pictures attitude.

Too embarrassed to return to her seat, Rachel wandered unsteadily up the aisle, holding seat backs for balance as she went. One empty seat lay before her at the extreme front of the car. Facing the open seat, with her back to Rachel, sat another elderly woman, not exactly a snappy dresser, wearing a black overcoat and what from the rear appeared to be a round, black bowler hat. Cotton candy curls of long gray hair cascaded down her shoulders from either side of the bowler. Rachel had little choice. She had to sit before she fell down again. So she slipped into the booth across from the woman. Their eyes met, and it was Rachel's turn to gasp. Below the bowler nestled a pair of bushy gray eyebrows, a pair of black horn-rimmed glasses thick as soda bottle bottoms, and a jungle of gray beard drawn out into two distinct points at its tips, dangling nearly two feet below the old gentleman's chin.

"You're not a woman!" Rachel slapped her fingers to her own lips, everlastingly too late. The man's thick glasses reflected her wide-eyed look of surprise. He appeared to smile, although it was difficult to tell with all of that beard in the way. The outer edges of the mossy hair seemed to curl ever so slightly toward his ears for a moment, and his magnified eyes narrowed kindly. "What I meant to say is . . ." she cleared her throat. "A *lot* of women . . . A lot of women ride this

train, don't they? Young women . . . girls, I mean.
Teenagers and so forth." She felt herself squirm. The
old gent said nothing, his owl-eye gaze returning to the
open window beside him.

Rachel, too, looked out the window, wondering
whether to say any more or simply fall out into the
aisle. Both would be equally humiliating. Then something caught her eye. The train had entered another
curve in its winding route, and the scenic window view
allowed passengers a glimpse of the track far ahead,
hatching through the flattened valley around them.
The train engine, only a few cars ahead of her own,
came into sight on the curve. But beyond the engine,
at a point near the horizon, she noticed a fuzzy white
blur. It appeared to be moving. Indeed, as the train
drew closer, the blob appeared to be jerking back and
forth. Rachel raised in her seat, squinting for a closer
look. Not only was the blob near the tracks, she realized, it was *on* the tracks. Bobbing first one direction,
then the other as if . . . as if . . . trapped. Something
was out there, trapped on the tracks.

She stood and held the windowsill for balance. Then
she leaned over the sill through the opening, allowing
the air outside the train to whip at her hair. The train
grew closer, the curve in the tracks grew tighter, the
blob became clearer and clearer. Without thinking, she
lunged dangerously out the window and filled her
lungs with the rushing air. And from somewhere deep
inside a cry sprang from her throat toward the train
engineer's open window.

"Stop this train! You've got to stop this train!"

CHAPTER 5

Elliot was at her side in seconds, his fingers squeezing her shirtsleeve.

"Goodness Agnes! What are you doing?" he groaned under his breath.

"We have to stop this train!" she said again. "Look!" She pointed out the window as Elliot jostled beside her for a better look. "There! Do you see it?" Elliot leaned over the windowsill into the rush of wind outside the train.

"It's . . . it's . . ." He squinted till his eyes nearly disappeared beneath his brow. "It's a goat."

"A goat?"

"Looks like it's got a leg stuck on a railroad tie or something."

"Will we miss it? The train, I mean . . . will it miss the goat?" she asked insistently.

"I'm sure it'll move once the train . . ."

But what if it was caught somehow, stuck on the track? The situation required quick thinking and quick action. Rachel knew she had experience in both, though Elliot liked to point out that her actions usually outran her brain by a mile. Apparently no one else had noticed the animal. Something had to be done, and quickly. She stretched across Elliot's back, snatched his hat and toppled it out the window.

"Rachel!" He grabbed at his sandy blonde hair, flipping in the breeze. But she shoved him aside.

"Stop! Stop!" She wailed until the two men guiding the train engine through the tight curve gave her their full attention, staring and pointing at her across the two-car expanse between the engine and her railcar. She seized the moment, waving wildly in the direction of Elliot's poor hat as it tumbled alongside the metal rails. "Someone's fallen from the train!"

Everyone in the railcar immediately rushed to the windows. And, just as quickly, the train shuddered madly as its merciless brakes froze against the wheels. Rachel heard the screams. She felt the jolt of a booth seat against her back. Two French teenagers flew past her in the aisle, landing in a heap near the wooden panels lining the front of the railcar. Sparks leapt from the rails beneath the window. A full fifteen seconds passed before the train finally rocked to a screeching halt. The wheels fell silent below the clamor of shouting voices surrounding her, some of which were shouting at *her*.

Already Elliot was on his knees helping the bearded woman whose wide body now blocked the aisle. Rachel struggled to her feet to peer through the window. Both engineers had left the train at a dead run in search of the lost passenger. And there, no more than twenty yards in front of the train engine's massive bulk of metal, stood the goat, staring blankly at all of the commotion. A fountain of fear and relief rushed through Rachel's body—relief that she had saved the goat, but fear of what would happen next.

Several people left the railcar to search for the fallen passenger who didn't exist. It didn't take long for Elliot's ratty hat to be found. And even less time passed before Elliot joined the cluster of passengers and engineers huddled beside the train, and reclaimed his hat.

"Yes, it's mine," he explained to one engineer. "It . . . well, I was at the window and suddenly it flew from my head."

So far so good. Rachel had not yet heard her name in any of the conversation. But there was still a lot of mopping up to do, and as much as she hated to, she would rescue Elliot.

"Oh, you're alive!" she cried, pushing her way past gawking passengers and flying down the railcar steps. "I thought we had lost you!" She wrapped him in her arms with the flair of a fine actress. "Are you all right?"

"Rachel . . ." He looked her square in the eyes.

"Silly me. Here I thought you had fallen from the train!" She moved her gaze past him and pretended to see the goat for the very first time. "But look! If you hadn't lost your hat, we might have all been killed by that poor, dumb animal blocking our path. You have saved us!" She faced the engineers. "It's . . . it's almost a miracle!" She clutched her hands to her chest. Then she nearly melted when the goat slowly wandered away from the track in search of greener weeds. It wasn't trapped at all.

Neither the engineers nor the passengers showed any interest in Rachel's miracle. A lot of yelling began, most of it in Hebrew. Rachel felt fortunate that she didn't speak the language. She did understand the hand signals, however, that waved her and Elliot away from the train. The two of them stood beneath the midday sun, silently watching the angry mob around them disappear into the railcars. Then, without so much as a whistle, the train eased forward and slowly chugged north. Without them.

Disbelief clutched her throat.

"They can't do this. They can't just leave us here to die. Wait!" She started to chase after the final railcar, but realized it was much too late for that. She turned around and moped back toward Elliot and his stony silence, while trying to look as sorrowful as possible without actually apologizing.

Elliot drew a long, slow breath through his nostrils. Then he let it all out in one burst, rattling his lips with a sound like a contented horse. His head tilted to one side, hat and all, and he smiled—despite their terrible predicament, he just smiled. And Rachel felt the unavoidable urge to strike out at him.

"What on earth do you find humorous about this situation!" She had no desire to hear an answer so she didn't offer her words as a question. They came out as more of a yell.

He clutched his hands to his chest, imitating Rachel's earlier dramatics.

"It's a miracle!" He dropped his arms. "Two miracles, actually. One—that no one was killed on that train.

And two—that no one on the train killed *us*. Since when did you acquire this great love for goats?" he asked, still smiling. "I thought you hated goats."

"I detest them. I despise them. They are nasty, smelly animals with coats like burlap and brains the size of walnuts."

"So why are we standing out here, watching the rear end of our train slip away, in the middle of Israel, in a valley as old as time . . . with a goat?"

Bleeaahhh! said the goat, which chose that moment to look at Rachel reproachfully.

Rachel set her jaw and said the first thing that came to mind. "Because . . . this goat reminds me of you! Except it has a bigger brain."

Elliot didn't answer. Instead he looked up and down the open valley before them, as if to get his bearings. Then he sat cross-legged near the train track watching the goat, which obviously had nowhere in particular to go and nothing important to do. It wandered unconsciously in small circles, choosing clumps of green to nibble. Everything about the dumb animal seemed unconscious, which probably accounted for its presence on the rail track in the first place. Finally, Elliot stole a glance at his space-age wristwatch.

"Well," he began, "we've got about three hours to figure out a way back to Qiryat Gat. Otherwise, we miss Nigel, he returns to the dig without us, Dad comes searching for us, assuming he has a clue where to start . . ."

"You're enjoying this, aren't you?" Rachel said accusingly. "It's now become some sort of personal challenge, hasn't it? You have everything you need—a problem and a deadline. I should think you'd be happy as a clam, stranded out here."

"We're not exactly stranded," Elliot replied. He motioned to the east where a cluster of buildings stood amid manicured farm fields and scrubby vegetation. "That's a *kibbutz*. Kind of a gigantic family farm operation." Not far beyond, an enormous satellite dish loomed above the valley floor like a giant white dinner plate turned sideways and framed with a spider web of metal struts and girders.

"What is that?"

"A television satellite dish." Elliot continued to survey the valley for a minute or two, clearly giving careful thought to something. Then he opened his satchel.

Rachel approached him. "A television station? Marvelous. Let me see . . . what say we tune in and catch the last half of 'Gilligan's Island,' shall we? Just pull out your little telly. I'll pop us some microwave popcorn." He barely glanced up from the guidebook now propped in his hands. This made her furious. "Yes, that's the ticket! Let's do a bit of leisure reading. Nothing like a relaxing read after having been popped from a train." She kicked at a dirt clod, causing the goat to buck away from the rail track. "And you . . ." she growled, turning to face the animal, "I suppose you think I've forgotten about you. I should pop you over the head."

"Doing a lot of popping, aren't you?" Elliot said from behind the guidebook cover.

She took a deep breath of surrender and sat next to

her cousin. "All this popcorn talk has made me hungry. I don't suppose you've got anything to eat in that Pony Express bag of yours."

Without a word, Elliot reached into the bag and fished out a candy bar. She grabbed it from his hand.

"Well, I'm certain I would never have seen this had we not been threatened with starvation!" She took a large bite the moment she had the wrapping open. Only then did she consider sharing it, which she would gladly do after she had eaten her fill. Meanwhile, Elliot traded his guidebook for another book in his bag. He flipped through the worn pages to the end, where a series of colorful maps resided. Rachel chomped off another bite of candy bar and peered over his shoulder. "That's Uncle Mason's Bible, isn't it? Are you planning to use the telly-station to contact angels now?"

"This *is* the Holy Land, Rachel. It makes sense to carry useful guidebooks along, even a guidebook as old as this." He thumped the center of a map labeled 'Lands of the Sea Peoples.' Then he pointed to the satellite dish. "Know where we are?"

"The Archeology Boy Wonder just informed me we're in the Holy Land," she snapped. The final piece of candy bar slid through her lips, leaving just enough chocolate on her fingers to wipe on the wrapper, which she tossed over her shoulder.

"Even better than that." He stood. His right arm swept across the horizon. "This is the Valley of Elah."

"What a relief! For a moment I thought you said the Valley of Elliot. That would have been a true disaster."

"Thousands of years ago this was Philistine country,"

he went on. "A great battle took place here. The Philistines set up camp along the hillsides." He motioned to a worn cliffside framing the valley along the west. "King Saul of Israel and his men camped over there, across the valley, somewhere just beyond the satellite dish . . . which wasn't there 3,000 years ago, of course."

Another boring archeology lecture in the making. Rachel didn't need a history lesson about some old battle—she needed a way home. And unless Elliot's growing story meant finding their way back to Cat Gut, she wanted no part of it.

He took several steps toward the television station. "That's when David showed up."

"David? David who? You're blabbering again. About the Flintstones."

"You've heard the story about David the shepherd boy, and how he slew the giant Goliath, champion of the Philistines, haven't you? I'm sure Aunt Lilia told you that one."

"Oh, I'm certain she has," Rachel said with heavy sarcasm. "She tells stories all the time, mostly about herself."

"This is where it happened—the battle between David and Goliath! Right where we're standing! Here, listen. I think it's in one of the books of Samuel." He flipped backward through the Bible pages.

"Samuel who?"

"Just Samuel. A judge in Israel over 3,000 years ago."

"Doesn't it strike you as odd that none of these people had a last name?" she challenged. "David . . .

Samuel . . . Goldfish the Giant. I doubt they ever got mail, not having proper last names and so forth. The postman wouldn't know who should receive what!" Elliot seemed a bit flustered at this line of questioning, so she pushed on. "And, yes—I know the story of the shepherd, tending his sheep, when along comes this giant hairy man with a spear who tries to run the lad through. And David is the hero who bonks the giant on the head with something . . . a coconut as I recall."

Elliot laughed aloud.

"Well, you've got the giant and spear part right. But the coconut must have come from too many episodes of 'Gilligan's Island.'" He read silently for a minute, then held up a finger. Another minute passed as he read to the end of the page and closed the Bible.

"Goliath was a Philistine warrior—and a giant as well—seven, maybe eight feet tall. Huge. He came to fight the Israelites with the modern weaponry and armor of the times, including a long heavy spear that was unlike most others. And David the shepherd boy bravely faced him in battle here in this valley, one-on-one, armed with only a hand sling and five stones from the *wadi* . . . the creek beds that flow with water through these areas in the rainy season."

Rachel ignored him by pretending to manicure her fingernails, although the idea of standing in the valley of a giant certainly caught her attention.

"Anyway, David used his sling, which probably wasn't more than a wide strap of leather, to sail a rock into the giant's forehead, and the rest is history. Like they say, 'The bigger they are . . .'"

" . . . The longer you talk," she cut him off. "Fascinating story, Wadi-Brain. But I fail to see how a tale about giants and sheepherders will help us return to Cat Gut by four o'clock. What I need from you is a giant *idea*, preferably one that involves neither sheep nor goats."

"Oh, that. I've already got that problem figured out."

"Do you," she snorted. "Just how do you propose we get back . . . ride sidesaddle on the goat?"

"No. We ride in style." Elliot waved over her shoulder, prompting Rachel to spin around and spot a cloud of dust roiling toward them on a makeshift road crossing the valley. Rolling along in front of the dust cloud was an old Jeep with no top and only one occupant.

"Who is that?" she asked.

"That," he smiled, "is our train ticket to Qiryat Gat. Right on time."

CHAPTER 6

Rachel stared as the Jeep drew nearer. Like most vehicles she had observed in their recent travels through the countryside, it was dirty, dented, and looked as though it shouldn't be running at all. A metal windshield frame rose behind the Jeep's cock-eyed hood, but it lacked one important item—a windshield. As a result, the driver's free-flowing head covering flapped in the breeze like he was riding a swift camel. She turned back to Elliot.

"Do you know this man?"

"Not yet," Elliot replied. "But we will in a moment." The Jeep reeled into a wide U-turn and circled them before its ungreased brakes screeched to a stop. The man behind the wheel adjusted his white head garb. Pushing his mustache aside, he revealed a gold tooth in a wide smile.

"Good day. You don't happen to be headed south, do you?" came Elliot's humble greeting.

The Jeep man's mouth opened, but the smile remained fixed on his face.

"I am returning home, to Lachish," he said in clear English. He stood in the Jeep, revealing the tails of his gray waistcoat, and surveyed the valley around them. The scene must have seemed quite odd to him—two kids and a goat lounging near an empty railroad track. "Did you miss the train to Qiryat Gat?"

"In a manner of speaking, yes," Rachel jumped in. "We're in a bit of a pickle, actually. We've taken a holiday from our research efforts at the archeological dig near Lachish, and a colleague is meeting us in Cat Gut, at the train station." *That should impress him*, she thought. "At any rate, the silly train schedule has boggled our plans a bit."

Elliot took one step forward as if to hide her in his shadow.

"To make a long story short . . . we sure could use a ride to Qiryat Gat, if you're going that way."

"I can take you to the train station. Please, get in."

"Thanks!" Elliot grabbed his satchel, tossed it in the backseat, then leapfrogged into the Jeep without opening the door. But Rachel didn't budge. She stood instead alongside the railroad track. Near the goat.

"This goat is yours?" asked the Jeep man.

"No," Elliot answered.

"Yes," Rachel corrected him. A remnant of candy bar wrapper hung from the goat's lower lip. The rest was inside somewhere. "I rescued this animal from certain death," she said, addressing Elliot. "We can't just leave it stranded here, like *we* were stranded here."

"This goat is the *reason* we're stranded here!" explained Elliot. He removed his wire-rimmed glasses and blew briefly on each lens to clear the dust. "So far, it's cost us the price of two train tickets and a candy bar. I get the feeling this is only the beginning. C'mon, Rachel."

The Jeep man sized up the animal nibbling weeds along the rail track.

"I think it is a pygmy goat. Much smaller than most breeds we have here." He reached over to open the passenger door for Rachel. The goat, sensing an offer it couldn't refuse, trotted over.

A shocked look crossed Elliot's face.

"We really don't own the goat . . . you don't need to . . ." he began. But before he could utter another word, the goat bounced past the open door and into his lap.

Mr. Gold Tooth laughed out loud.

"Congratulations. You now own a goat."

Gleefully, Rachel hopped into the front seat next to the Jeep man.

"Well, this has worked out jolly good, hasn't it?"

"Jolly good," Elliot mumbled. "Maybe we can find a couple of hitchhiking cattle along the way, too."

"So, your name is Rachel," their new acquaintance said as he steered the military-looking Jeep back toward the unmarked road.

Rachel hesitated.

"Why, yes. How did you know that?"

"I just said your name a second ago, remember?" Elliot grunted from the back of the Jeep where he wrestled to keep the goat under control.

"Yes, right." She squinted against the dust and wind blowing through the missing windshield.

"My name is Aron Segal." The Jeep man offered her his hand, which she shook firmly.

"And I'm Elliot Conner." Elliot reached his free hand over the backseat. "Pleased to meet you Mr. Segal. You don't know *how* pleased we are to meet you. This would have been a long walk."

Aron Segal's gold tooth appeared.

"Especially with your new goat." Rachel caught a glimpse of Elliot's faint smile and knew he was pleased that the goat was safe.

They rode for some time, with only the sound of wind through the empty windshield frame as conversation. When the road grew less bumpy, Elliot finally struck up a discussion with their soft-spoken driver. Even riding in the back seat of a creaky Jeep wrestling a goat, Elliot had a knack for finding common ground with strangers. Usually he got people to talk about themselves and convinced them he was interested. Rachel envied him for it, of course, but sometimes it worked in her favor.

"Is it always so green here in the lowlands this time of year?"

"Not always," Aron replied. "The *yoreh* came this season. And when the *yoreh* come, the *Shephelah*, the lowland, springs to life again."

"*Yoreh?*" Rachel echoed. "Are they any relation to the *moshav* guy who owns everything?"

Elliot replied with a puzzled look. "The *yoreh* are the early season rains that fall this time of year," he explained. He nudged the goat from the seat to the floorboard and leaned forward to address their new chauffeur. "Were you visiting the *kibbutz* here in the valley?"

"Yes," said the Jeep driver. "I often purchase grain from the *kibbutz* for my turkey farm. I imagine my turkeys have awakened you each morning—they are quite noisy, and my farm is less than two kilometers from the dig at Lachish."

"You mean you live beside the hula-hoop-and-long-underwear building?" asked Rachel.

"The hothouses," came Elliot's interpretation.

Aron smiled.

"Yes. My farm and the *moshav* surround the base of Tel Lachish. I would be happy for you to visit."

"I'd like that," Elliot said. "Although we're a bit limited on time, I'm afraid. My father only has a few more days at Lachish before we return to the States. And I was really hoping to do some artifact-hunting near Adullam, in the hills."

"Ah . . . *Tel esh-Sheik Madhkur*," mumbled Aron.

Rachel leaned over the seat and whispered in Elliot's ear over the windy ride.

"Am I supposed to answer that? Did he say just something, or was he just clearing his throat?"

"Adullam," continued Aron, repeating his response in English this time. "The stronghold of David. You are interested in the caves, I assume?"

"Right." Elliot shifted positions in the backseat so as not to be crowded by the fidgeting goat. "Are you familiar with that area? I understand there is an old cistern just north of there, too."

Aron nodded. "I am impressed by your knowledge.

Few visitors know of the cistern."

Elliot shrugged. "I like to do a little reading about the places we visit, that's all."

"I can arrange for you to travel there if you wish."

"Yes, I wish!" Elliot bolted forward in his seat.

"Tomorrow. Come down to my turkey farm in the morning and I will show you the way."

"This is great! Rachel, isn't this great?"

Rachel was more concerned with the soreness developing in her rear than she was about caves and cisterns.

"Simply grand," she said flatly, rubbing at her hip, which was sore from bumping over a trackless road in a roofless Jeep.

"Or," Aron went on, "perhaps you should speak with the Englishman at the Lachish dig. He also wishes to visit the caves at Adullam."

"Englishman?" Rachel perked up. "You mean Nigel Chatsworth?"

"Yes. He stopped by my farm late yesterday to inquire about the caves."

By now the stairstep buildings of Cat Gut had risen up to greet them, and they soon reached the railway station they had left only a few hours earlier. Aron Segal parked his Jeep and helped them unload their belongings. And their goat.

"It was a pleasure meeting you," Elliot offered. "And thanks again for the ride."

"Yes, thank you," echoed Rachel. She knew this man had saved them from certain trouble—trouble she had created.

"You were serious about the visit to your farm and to Adullam?" Elliot added.

"Certainly. I shall see you in the morning." He revved the Jeep engine, which sputtered nearly as badly as the old supply truck, then he bid them farewell with a wave. Suddenly, he stomped the brakes and called out over his shoulder with a gold-tooth smile: "You have a fine goat there!" Then he and the Jeep disappeared.

Rachel put her hands to her hips.

"Well, that was sporting of him, to carry us here. But turkeys?" she shuddered. "How could anyone spend his life playing nursemaid to a bunch of turkeys? Turkeys are worse than goats."

"It's called a 'rafter' of turkeys, actually, not a 'bunch.' Look Rachel, the man gave us a ride, didn't he? Just think of him as . . . as a livestock rancher. Some ranchers raise cattle. He raises turkeys."

"How unpleasant."

"Speaking of unpleasant," Elliot said, "what do you plan to do with *your* livestock?"

Rachel looked hard at the four-legged stink bomb tethered to the end of the guide rope in Elliot's grasp.

"I shall take it to the dig," she answered without hesitation. "The people there shall care for it. It might be useful, you know. Goats make milk or something, don't they?"

"Have you ever tasted raw goat's milk?" Elliot's face screwed into a grimace.

"Yes, I believe I have," she snapped. "And I believe it was in some forsaken country at some dig. At your bidding, as I recall. Disgusting. No matter. The workers will drink it."

"You know what Dad will say . . . 'It's your animal, you care for it.' "

"You archeologists are a responsible lot," she sneered.

Elliot grinned.

"Well, we have a long wait ahead of us." He surveyed the parking area searching for a spot of shade. "Nigel isn't scheduled to be back for at least an hour or more."

"Just so we are gone before the train returns," Rachel said slowly. "I have no desire to see anyone riding that train again in my entire life." She took a deep breath, held it, then let it out in a burst, along with her decision to admit her mistake. "I know, I know," she began, holding her hands up in front of her, "it was foolish of me to stop the train like that. Dangerous, in fact. Particularly for the likes of an animal such as this."

"You did what you thought was right. Given the choice, I wish you hadn't thrown my hat out the train window. But, hey, you saved a goat, right?"

"Right. Marvelous."

A whining engine broke her train of thought. She turned to see the rickety supply truck, with its swaying canvas cover and bouncing British driver, pull into the train station. Nigel had returned. Rachel hurried to meet him, waving and smiling and waiting for just the right moment to mention the goat.

"You're early! Everything went well in town, I trust," Rachel spoke up. She added a contrived giggle, hoping

Nigel wouldn't think her too forward. Dr. Chatsworth nodded his head but didn't answer. His attention was focused on the rearview mirror and the back end of the supply truck. Rachel studied his expression, the tiny beads of sweat dimpling his close-shaven face, the concerned squint in his eyes. For the first time since she had met him, Nigel made her feel uncomfortable. Downright creepy, in fact. Each glance in the rearview mirror made Rachel want to look over her own shoulder, in case someone was sneaking up from behind.

"Was there a problem in Cat Gut? Or with the truck perhaps?"

"No, nothing really. I finished my errands early," Nigel answered with a half-smile. He seemed to be in a bit of a rush. "Shall we be off then?"

"Uhhh . . . yes, I suppose we should." She paused.

"Where is Elliot?" he broke in somewhat sharply. This was the opening Rachel had waited for.

"Elliot? Yes, well . . . he's right over there with . . . uh . . . you see, we've picked up something from the train ride to take back to camp—if that's not a bother."

Nigel tried peering past her to the train station but Rachel purposely blocked his view. He gave the supply truck horn several beeps, motioning for Elliot to hurry over.

"Souvenir of some sort?" Nigel mumbled, and again he gave the horn an impatient tap.

"Souvenir?" Rachel glanced back at Elliot. He had gathered the guide rope in his arms and was tugging with little success at the animal. She felt the smile broaden across her face. Nigel was making this much easier than she had imagined. "Yes, that's it. A one-of-a-kind souvenir. A real treasure. We just *couldn't* leave it on the train." That much was true. Rachel would have been *arrested* for leaving the goat on the train, if the angry mob of passengers hadn't strangled her first, that is.

"Well, all right then." His impatience had reached a level that could almost be called impolite. "Toss it up front here. One of you will need to hold it on your lap."

Rachel felt a nervous tickle cross her brow. "Uh, it's a bit big to hold, actually. Perhaps we can put it in the back?" She hoped the cringe in her voice wasn't too obvious. And she *would* tell him that their souvenir was a goat. She really would. But just not yet.

"Ohhhh!" Nigel groaned and squeezed his forehead briefly. Then he grabbed at the door handle. "I'll help you load it then. We really do need to be on our way!"

"No, no! Stay right where you are. Elliot and I can pop it in the back and we'll soon be on our way!" She rushed back to Elliot, who by now had jerked and goaded the poor animal to the rear of the truck. Rachel pulled back one side of the canvas curtains draped across the truck bed and waited for Elliot to load the goat. But from the look on Elliot's face, Rachel knew she would be waiting a long time.

"Well, up with it then," she directed. "And be quick. Nigel seems to be in a rush."

Elliot's expression tightened like a rope in a fierce tug-of-war, stretching into what Rachel recognized as downright stubbornness—something rarely seen in her cousin.

"Well?" she pushed.

"Well?" came his daring reply. The loose end of the guide rope tethered around the goat's neck slithered from his hand. His arms rose and crossed, setting a clear barrier between him and Rachel. "Look, Rachel. You wanted to save the goat, so we saved the goat. We risked arrest and possible torture at the hands of angry train commuters. You insisted we haul this dumb animal back here at great inconvenience to everyone involved, including us. Now you expect me to hoist him into the truck by myself?"

"Him? How do you know it's a him?"

"Take my word for it, Rachel. This is a *billy* goat. A *him*."

Nigel blasted the truck horn, sending an angry chill up Rachel's spine.

"Oh, you really are a twist," she muttered to Elliot. "I ask one small favor and you act as though I've made you a slave for life." Gingerly, she patted the floor of the truck bed and whispered, "Here, goaty, goaty. Jump on up into the truck."

"*Bleeaahhh!*"

"Shhhhh! Why do you keep making that awful noise?"

"That's what goats do, Rachel. They make awful noises."

The sound of the driver's door opening and Nigel's boots grinding against the graveled lot gave Rachel the humility she needed to sputter out the next few words. "Help me lift the goat, Elliot . . . please?"

The eternal Elliot grin awakened as he leaned one

shoulder against the truck bed frame and uncrossed his arms just long enough to adjust his hat. He said nothing but obligingly hoisted the goat's dangerous rear end over the low rear gate into the truck. Rachel strained with the front end, tossed the guide rope aside and hastily drew the curtain across the bed frame. And not a moment too soon. Nigel's distressed face peered around the back of the truck.

"Are we loaded now?" he asked, with controlled irritation.

"Oh yes, quite," Rachel clucked. "Let's be off."

The ride back to camp seemed much bumpier and Rachel feared Nigel might ask what it was in the back that clomped and jolted so as they drove. He forged ahead through dips instead of around them, cornered tightly on the curves, and generally drove like a madman until Cat Gut was no longer in sight behind them. Then he seemed to loosen up a bit. Several tugs at his own shirt collar relaxed his appearance. Rachel felt as if she were trapped between twin brothers born twenty years apart. Finally he spoke.

"So then, how was the train? And what sort of souvenir did you find in your travels?"

"Souvenir?" Elliot answered with a touch of bewilderment. He looked into Rachel's eyes. She stared back at him with daggers, but he rushed ahead anyway. "Does he mean the billy go—"

Elliot's muddled reply sounded like someone yodeling with a mouthful of Cheerios. Rachel's hand covered his mouth.

"I believe what Elliot's trying to say," she offered, her fingers pressed over his open mouth, "is that we were *beside* ourselves when we found it. We . . ."

Elliot pushed her arm away. Obviously he realized that Nigel had not heard the full story.

"You mean you didn't tell him about the goat?" he blurted out.

Nigel eased his foot from the gas pedal.

"The *what*?"

"The goat. Standing on the railroad track. And the turkey farmer who . . . I thought Rachel told you all of this."

"Actually, no," he said in a low, firm tone. His eyes remained focused on the road.

It was time to come clean.

"Well, all right, then," Rachel snapped. "We've a goat. A billy goat, to be precise, assuming Elliot Conner, Master Veterinarian, knows his 'hims' and 'hers.' I saved the smelly thing before the train turned it into goat yogurt!" She swiveled to face Elliot. "There, I've said it. I hope you're pleased as punch."

Nigel made a low choking sound in his throat which, to Rachel's relief, grew into a chuckle.

"A goat, you say?" He chuckled again. "Well . . . I imagine you and your train companions had quite a return trip to Qiryat Gat. Smelly things, goats." He chuckled again.

"Then you're not angry?" Rachel asked. She had no intention of bringing up the turkey farmer, nor of correcting Nigel about his assumption that the goat rode the train.

"Not at all. It's your goat, not mine." He paused. "You'll have to take care of it, you know."

Rachel suspected Nigel's calm response had little to do with the goat and more to do with his relief at escaping whatever he seemed to be running from back in Cat Gut. No matter. He didn't appear angry with her. That's all that counted. She slipped Elliot a satisfied smile.

"See, Elliot? I told you he wouldn't mind."

CHAPTER 7

"Tomorrow? I think not!" Rachel warned, with a rub at her rear. "Only three hours ago we were in Cat Gut. My bottom won't bear another trip so soon in that old supply truck. Especially to someplace called 'Adullam.' It all sounds so . . . so *dull*."

Elliot dropped the brim of his hat to counter the red glow of the setting sun and smiled at her attempted pun.

"It wouldn't seem right without you. Besides, I'm sure Nigel would like you to come along. You've gotten pretty chummy with him—at least you've managed to hoodwink him out of his tea lately."

"I'll take that as a compliment," Rachel replied in her purest British accent. "By the way, I asked Nigel about that scar on his wrist."

"You didn't."

"Certainly I did. I told him you were curious about it," she added playfully.

"What did he say?"

"He told me he injured it playing rugby. I'm not sure I believe him."

"Rugby can be a pretty rough sport," Elliot observed.

"Quite. But one doesn't use knives or hatchets to play! No . . . something else happened to him. And I intend to find out what it was." She plopped to the ground, pressed her back against one of Lachish's many ruined walls, and shaded her eyes with one hand, as if saluting Elliot. Darkness had nearly fallen at the dig. "So . . . what's so great about Dullsville?"

"Adullam," Elliot reminded her. "Well, it's in the hill country, for one thing. We can spend the day hiking."

Rachel drew her mouth into a sneer. "Lovely."

Elliot paused for a moment. "I did a little reading before dinner this evening . . ." he began.

"That's why you wear those silly glasses, you know. You've nearly ruined your eyes with all that reading. You don't see any glasses propped on my face, do you? I save my eyes for more important things. Like snooping."

Elliot cleared his throat. "As I was saying," he went on, "I did some reading about the history of this area, particularly the hill country just north of here. Remember the story I told you earlier . . . about David and the giant?"

Rachel sighed dramatically.

"Yes, I remember . . . you were droning on about it just before Jeepers picked us up."

"Who?"

"Jeepers. Mr. Gobble-Gobble." Elliot looked confused. "The Turkey Keeper!" she crowed.

"You mean Aron?"

"Oh, whatever! I prefer to call him Jeepers. It's much

easier to remember, especially since he drives that bombed-out Jeep."

Elliot shook his head as if to clear his brain of her interruptions. "Anyway . . . David and his armies spent lots of time roaming the hills near Adullam. There aren't many formal digs in that area . . . but I'll bet it's loaded with artifacts."

"So you intend to find them, is that it?"

A slow grin lifted his cheeks. "Something like that."

She remained silent for a moment, then a laugh gurgled up inside her.

"Goodnesss Agnes! What's so funny? That's the third time you've laughed for no reason since we got back to the dig!"

"I can't help thinking," Rachel answered through her giggles, "about the look on Uncle Mason's face when we unloaded that goat from the supply truck this afternoon." She noticed Elliot trying to hide a smile, probably thinking the same thought.

"You heard what he said," Elliot warned her from behind a grin.

"Yes, I know, I know." She sat as straight as she could and threw out her jaw in an attempt to imitate Uncle Mason. Then in a low, round voice she bellowed, " 'That goat is your responsibility now—it is up to you to care for it.' He sounded just like you, only louder. You would have thought we'd dragged home an infant in diapers the way he acted."

Elliot didn't answer; instead, he looked eastward toward the Judean hills, awash in the orange twilight. Rachel studied him silently and marveled at how he resembled Uncle Mason—not so much in looks, but in the way he thought about things. Like the goat, for example. It truly was her responsibility, and she should never have stopped the train to get it. Uncle Mason had reminded her of that very fact shortly after Elliot told him the entire story of how they came to have a goat in the first place. Elliot had insisted they tell the truth, then he shared the blame for ruining a good train ride for all the tourists—foolishness on his part, as far as Rachel was concerned. Funny thing was, Uncle Mason would have done the same thing.

"You're serious, aren't you? About riding to Dullsville tomorrow, I mean." Elliot nodded his reply. "We can take the goat then?"

Her question broke his trance. "Goodness Agnes! Why would we take the goat?"

"A bit peckish, aren't we?" she teased. "That's two 'Goodness Agneses' in a row. I don't know why we would take the goat. As a good-luck charm, perhaps."

Elliot adjusted his wire-rimmed glasses and slowly folded his arms across his chest while cocking his head to look at her with only one eye—the "lizard eye," as Rachel called it. Elliot's "lizard-eye" look made lying next to impossible, although she had managed to skirt around it before. But not this time.

"It's like this," she confessed. "I've never really had a pet. Mother wouldn't allow it . . . or rather, Mother's schedule wouldn't allow it. As a result, I'm not terribly keen on animals, or on certain people for that matter. But when I saw that goat on the railway track, some-thing inside me whispered, 'This is the pet you never had.'" She stole a glance in the goat's direction. It stood near the barracks rubbing its head against a wedge of rock.

"I assume you're going somewhere with this story?"

"I've owned this animal four hours, and already I wish I had never had it! It is noisy and rude. It cares for no one but itself and is concerned only with filling its belly. And it smells. It smells bad."

"You've just described every goat on earth. So—"

"So," Rachel butted in, flopping her arms into her lap, "I propose we transport the sorry bag of bones as far as the turkey farm and present it to Jeepers. As a gift, of sorts."

"Mmmmm . . ." Elliot tipped his hat in thought.

"I saw the gleam in those green eyes of yours! You've something sneaky in mind, haven't you?" No one recognized sneaks quite as quickly as she did. It was an acquired talent, born from years of practice.

"Aron's farm *is* on the way to Adullam. And every farm needs at least one goat, right? He might even give us something in return."

"Like a trade of some sort? Money, perhaps! Or jewelry!" Suddenly the ride to Dullsville didn't seem so bumpy after all.

"I'm thinking we could swap the goat for the favor he offered."

Rachel purposely rolled her eyes and groaned loudly.

"Like what? A stroll through the turkey pens? I say we *sell* the goat. There's nothing else Jeepers has that we could possibly use."

"He has the experience of spending a lifetime here in

Israel. And he has a Jeep. He's offered to show us around the hill caves. No telling what we'd find there."

"Snakes. We would find snakes. I would rather have a dumb old goat than a smart snake."

"I'm talking artifacts here—priceless antiquities!" Elliot said excitedly.

"Oh, no! You're not going to trade my goat for some archeological twitter." She wasn't sure what 'antiquities' meant—but it didn't sound like jewelry.

Before Elliot could muster an answer, Uncle Mason's booming voice bounced from the nearby mess hall kitchen.

"Elliot! Rachel! Tea's on!"

Immediately Rachel jumped to her feet. "That's my cue. Come on."

In the mess hall, Uncle Mason and Dr. Cunningham lounged around the small wooden table where dig site meals and boring discussions took place. Supper dishes still laid strewn across the kitchen counter, except for those stacked carelessly on one corner of the table. At the table's center, a steaming hot teakettle piped away, filling the mess hall with the sweet aroma of fine British tea. The two archeologists had scarcely moved an inch since supper, locked in yet another boring discourse about pieces of who-knows-what dug from the ground that afternoon.

"Well, at least we've found a sword blade and several spear shaft fragments," Uncle Mason was saying. "That should help hold Nigel's interest a little."

"Yes, quite," Dr. Cunningham answered. "But he seems to have taken a special interest in the ostraca finds. "The richness of the ink . . . and the smooth pottery finish . . . definitely superior artifacts. High quality." The older man's brow furrowed over his tea cup. "If I might make a suggestion, Mason, I believe you should consider transporting the ostraca you've uncovered to the Rockefeller Museum in Jerusalem immediately. I fear for their safety here."

"Really?" Uncle Mason seemed shocked.

"Oh, yes. We've had quite a rash of losses the past year or so. Black marketeers and all that rot. Middle Eastern artifacts are very popular, you know. Several of the dig sites we worked on this summer lost some priceless items."

Uncle Mason shook his head and refilled Dr. Cunningham's tea cup. The wiry archeologist warmed his hands around the cup for a minute, then continued.

"Most of the thefts are reported from the field, often from active dig sites, although a few pieces actually disappeared from museums. Including the Rockefeller Museum," he added, unable to hide his distress. He seemed to take the losses personally. "I can't imagine what would possess someone to rob the archeological community, and the public as well, by stealing pieces of history. And for a mere thousand or so British pounds . . . or dollars, in your case, Mason."

"How awful," Rachel said. She used the opportunity to slip not only into the conversation, but into the tea line as well, pouring herself a cup as she clucked her tongue in disgust at the very idea. They ignored her, of course, but she figured her comment had earned her the right to tea.

"Well, we can pack our finds first thing tomorrow morning and send a runner to Jerusalem."

"I can arrange for Nigel to make the trip. That way we can avoid any local workers who might have black market connections. It's not that I don't trust the workers, mind you, it's just that a British archeologist in an American supply truck poses less concern."

The brim of Elliot's hat bumped softly against Rachel's hair. "Looks like we just found transportation to Aron's farm," he whispered in her ear.

"Nigel visited the Museum two weeks ago," Dr. Cunningham added. "He tells me he has additional research to conduct there on the Bronze Age collection, so I'm certain he won't mind the trip."

Uncle Mason's full grin appeared. "We'll send him, then. I understand we've got a rainshower brewing, anyway. Tomorrow may be a slow day."

Elliot stepped up to the table. "Uh . . . Dad? Since Nigel will be headed north, would it be okay if Rachel and I rode along? I'd like to do a little hiking in the hill country, around Adullam."

Uncle Mason peered over his tea cup, first at Elliot, then at Rachel. "So . . . the clouds aren't the only things brewing. My guess is you two have a little expedition planned, mmmm?"

"Something like that," Elliot shrugged. "Just a couple places I want to check out."

"The first place to check is Nigel—if it's okay with him, you're both welcome to go."

"Thanks, Dad. We can help pack up before breakfast."

"*You* can pack all you want," Rachel quickly pointed out. "I, however, have no intention of watching the sun come up in the morning."

"Oh, you'll be up," Elliot assured her.

"Doing what?"

He rapped his fist against the wall of the mess hall, then cupped his hand behind his ear. Through the walls came a faint but unmistakable sound.

Bleeaahhh! Bleeaahhh!

Elliot tipped his dingy hat in her direction. "Feeding the four-legged garbage disposal."

CHAPTER 8

"Hiking pack? Check." Rachel slapped at the travel pack strapped around her waist. "Dry socks?" she said, continuing through her checklist. "Check. Canteen? Check. Dirt-digger hat Uncle Mason insists I wear that makes me look as ridiculous as Elliot? Check."

"Rachel," Elliot interrupted, "this is a day trip, not a six-week wilderness hike. Just take what you need for a few hours of hiking in the hills."

"Really?" she said, sizing up the Pony Express bag clinging to Elliot's shoulder like an overstuffed pillow. "You're one to talk. Do you plan to carry that awful bag or are we pulling a wagon with us?"

"I need everything in this bag . . . camera, tools, empty artifact bag, journal . . ."

"Oh, certainly. Bring that diary of yours so you can write down each time you complain how heavy that bag is. Lovely idea." She returned to her list. "Hairbrush? Check. Candy bars—for me only? Check." She glanced into the back of the supply truck. "Goat? Check."

Bleeaahhh!

"Oh, bleeaahhh yourself! By evening you'll be bleating a new tune, living with Jeepers and hoping the Mr. Moshav fellow sees fit to give you something to eat. You're lucky I fed you at all this morning—I could have slept fifteen extra minutes, you know."

Rachel had barely finished scolding the goat when Nigel approached them carrying a large briefcase and a smaller shoulder bag—Elliot's twin, Mr. Pony Express Bag Number Two.

"Looks like we're on the road again, at least for a bit," he said. "Hop in and I'll drive you to the *moshav*."

"We'll be meeting him, then?" Rachel asked hopefully.

Elliot threw her a questioning look. "Meeting who?"

"Mr. Moshav."

"The *moshav* isn't a 'him.' It's an 'it.' It's the turkey farm . . . more or less."

"Of course. I knew that," Rachel quipped, not wanting to seem foolish in front of Nigel. How disappointing! She had imagined the Moshav to be a rich, powerful ruler of some sort, possibly with a jeweled turban swirled around his bald head and wearing slippers with curly toes. Meeting him would have been the highlight of this otherwise boring stint in the middle of nowhere. Instead, he was nothing more than a yard full of loud, ugly birds herded by a gold-toothed farmer who wore a waistcoat like George Washington's.

"You can ride in the back if you like . . . with the goat," Nigel added with a laugh. He certainly was chipper this morning, obviously looking forward to his trip to the museum in Jerusalem.

"We could just walk, you know," suggested Elliot. "It's

only a kilometer or two down to the farm."

"Oh, no trouble at all," Nigel assured him. "I can drop you at the farm. Or, if you like, you two are welcome to ride on with me. I'll be passing near Adullam. That is where you plan to hike isn't it, near the caves?"

"Right," Elliot replied, taking Nigel's bags. "But I'm counting on our turkey farmer to drive us into the hill country—maybe even give us some inside information on good artifact-hunting areas. Who knows what we'll find."

"*I* know what we'll find," snapped Rachel. "Snakes." She shooed the goat deeper into the supply truck's canvas cover, then mounted the tailgate and climbed in. Elliot followed, hefting Nigel's briefcase and bag along with his own.

After several attempts, Nigel finally coaxed the engine to life. He forced the truck into first gear and coasted down the dig site's sloping hillside. Rachel used her travel bag like a fanny pack to protect against the barrage of bumps the supply truck managed to find. Just before reaching the main road, however, the old army surplus truck found one final rollicking bump that sent her, Elliot, the goat, and everyone's belongings sprawling across the truck bed. The canvas covering surrounding them nearly rattled loose from its metal-pole framework.

"Sorry!" Nigel's voice called out from the passenger compartment. "Everyone all right back there?"

"Fine!" yelled Elliot as he crawled to the rear of the truck bed to retrieve his hat.

"Fine?" Rachel growled at Elliot. "He drives like a

madman! We're fortunate he hasn't killed us all in this four-wheeled junkpile!" She rubbed the spot on her hip where Nigel's bag had landed and began searching for her candy bars among the scattering of books, bags, tools and hiking provisions now sliding loose in the truck bed. Two lay near the zippered opening of her travel bag; two had tumbled from the bag into a pile with Elliot's camera equipment. The fifth candy bar poked from just above the goat's hairy chin like a fat cigar.

Rachel felt an angry gasp rise from her throat. "Give me that, you walking washrag!" she wailed. Without thinking, she rose to her knees and lunged at the animal as the last bite of candy bar disappeared into its toothy grin. The truck bed floor met her fall with a painful thud, cushioned only by a leather-bound book lying where she landed. Moaning dramatically, she reached beneath her chest to find Elliot's journal—his secret diary—tucked neatly into her hand. What luck! Her opportunity to snoop into her brainy cousin's thoughts had tumbled right into her lap! Or, in this case, her lap had tumbled onto *it*.

She tried to forget about the lost candy bar and concentrated instead on pulling her travel bag toward her, careful not to reveal the leather book in her grasp. A quick flip of her wrist sent the journal into the bag, which she zipped immediately.

As Nigel gradually slowed the dusty vehicle to a stop, one of the long, white hula-hoop buildings appeared behind the truck's canvas cover. Jeepers' turkey farm lay just ahead.

"Look, we're almost to Jeepers' place. Let me sort this mess out," Rachel offered. She helped Elliot gather up several empty artifact bags, a couple of books, and a flash unit for his camera. Rushing to repack the spilled travel bags might fool Eagle-Eye Elliot into thinking his journal was safe. She couldn't be *too* helpful, though, or he might suspect something.

Jeepers, whom Elliot insisted she call Aron, met them at the truck's rear bumper to help unload their bags. He wore the same clothing he had worn the previous day.

"I'm delivering two packages of trouble," Nigel called out to the farmer with his likable charm. "Three, actually. I hope you were expecting them."

"Three?" Jeepers peered into the truck bed as he offered Rachel assistance in climbing over the tailgate.

"We've brought the goat," began Rachel's sales pitch. "Every good turkey farm needs a goat, doesn't it? They are clean, quiet . . . did I mention they keep a place picked up? One day with this goat and you'll not have a single candy bar littering the turkey pasture, or whatever you call it." Elliot's eyes shot bullets at her. "Well, enough about us," she went on. She drew a deep breath and closed her eyes. "How I do love the sound of gobbling. Tell me, have your turkeys produced a lot of milk this season?"

Jeepers smiled a pleasant smile and said nothing, a trait Elliot often described as "the wisdom of silence." It was a wisdom Elliot said Rachel should practice, but didn't.

"You'll see that they arrive home safely, I trust," Nigel called. "I'm headed to Jerusalem for the day and shan't return until late."

A silent nod and waving hand from the turkey farmer sent Nigel on his merry way, leaving the trio and their highly advertised goat standing at the road's edge.

Jeepers was the first to speak.

"Welcome to B'nai Lachish *moshav*," he said with a sweep of his arm. "Our land belongs to Israel, and our people belong to the God of our fathers."

"It's very kind of you to invite us," Elliot answered. "And thanks again for the ride back to the dig yesterday. I doubt we could have made the trip without your help."

Aron's gold tooth sparkled through his mustache.

"Would you like something to drink before traveling on to Adullam?"

"Oh, that would be simply—" Rachel began with images of tea cups in her mind.

"No, thank you, anyway," came Elliot's overriding answer. "We've already intruded on your hospitality." That was Elliot—always the diplomat, even when there was tea to be had.

"Very well." Jeepers turned to face north, where a patchwork of green and chalk-colored hills lay along the horizon. "There is a small road just east of the farm that will lead you to Adullam. Follow it for fifteen kilometers, where you will cross the main highway to Hebron. Keep going until this road forks. Take the right fork and continue on for ten kilometers. You will see the ruins and their surrounding caves. The cistern you spoke of lies just north beyond a small highway, near the road's end." His hand emerged from his waist-coat pocket with a jingling key ring. "Here are the keys to the Jeep," he said calmly. He placed the keys in Elliot's palm.

"Goodness Agnes!" Elliot blurted. "You mean . . . you want us to just take the Jeep? By ourselves?"

"I will not be able to accompany you today. You have driven before?"

Rachel knew *she* hadn't, unless driving around the block a few times in her mother's car and running over the neighbor's mailbox counted.

"Uh . . . sure. Dad has me shuttle artifacts between dig sites sometimes. But . . ."

Rachel had heard all she needed to hear. Elliot could drive and Jeepers had offered keys. This day had adventure written all over it. She stepped in front of Elliot, snatched the keys from his hand and pocketed them before Jeepers could change his mind.

"We'll take it," she smiled with all of her charm. "Now, about the goat. He is for sale if you're interested. We have a fair offer from one of the dig workers, but nothing is final. At least not yet."

Elliot slipped her a hidden jab in the ribs with his elbow, then spoke.

"He's yours, if you'll have him. I'm afraid an active dig is no place for an active goat. Would there be a place for him here at the *moshav*?"

Jeepers seemed genuinely pleased. As he should— Elliot had just given him a free goat.

"Yes. He will prosper here. Thank you." The farmer

nodded slowly. "Does he have a name?"

"No."

"Yes!" Rachel shouted. He was her goat, after all. She had a right to name him before Elliot gave him away.

"I've named him . . . his name is . . ." Elliot crossed his arms and adjusted his wire-rimmed glasses so the "lizard eye" focused directly on her forehead. She said the first thing that came to mind. " . . . Ichabod."

Jeepers pursed his lips politely, as if considering the name.

"Then that will be his American name. Should he ever be called to read at temple, however, he will need a Hebrew name."

The goat approached Jeepers with a dull stare in his sad moon eyes.

Bleeaahhh!

Jeepers smiled. "His Hebrew name shall be Selah."

"Selah?" repeated Rachel.

"Yes. It is a musical term from the psalms of David—a good name for such a musical goat, eh?" He patted Selah's bony head. "The Jeep is there," he said with a nod. "And the road to Adullam lies there." His finger pointed east of the farm. "It is best to travel only in the daylight."

"Don't worry," Elliot promised. "We plan to be back well before dark."

Rachel found herself seated next to Elliot, who seemed almost comfortable in the driver's seat. He started the vehicle without a problem, but killed the engine several times until he became familiar with the loose clutch pedal. The short distance between the farm and the main road took five minutes to cover and included a great deal of jolting and jerking, but finally they were on their way.

Just beyond the sound of gobbling turkeys, the road began to wind slowly upward. It followed a straight course through one of several shallow valleys ringing the low hillsides. A light breeze rustled the leaves of orchard trees and yellow wildflowers on either side of the road. Spotty patches of tall cedars, rising like furry green rockets, dotted the shoulders of the hills before them. Soon they reached the highway Jeepers had mentioned. Elliot checked traffic, then edged the Jeep across the pavement to rejoin the graveled dirt road on the other side. Smoothly, he shifted the gears on the squeaky old Jeep, keeping one hand on the steering wheel, one on the stick shift poking from the floor, one foot on the gas pedal, and the other resting on the clutch, ready to press it whenever he changed gears.

"Why didn't you tell me you could drive?" Rachel harped. "Had I known, we could have made a run to town for tea and biscuits. I could be strolling through some quaint little shop in Cat Gut instead of thumping over chalk roads in search of snakes."

"I can't drive, really."

"Oh? What do you call steering a Jeep down a road . . . volleyball?"

"It's a little like rubbing your stomach and patting your head at the same time, working the clutch and everything," Elliot explained. Suddenly he slammed the Jeep to a lurching halt.

"What are you doing!" Rachel exclaimed.

"Be right back." Elliot twisted the key to stop the engine and jumped from the Jeep. "I saw something shiny flash over there, at the base of the hillside. Let me check it out."

Rachel moaned in disgust, but already Elliot was too far away to hear. Then a thought struck her. Finally! A moment alone—just her and Elliot's diary. She quietly slipped the leather journal from her bag, careful to click open the golden latch without disturbing the bookmark hiding within its pages. Odd . . . Elliot never used real bookmarks—only old slips of paper or envelopes. Nor did she remember any flashy gold latch. Cradling the book in her lap with one hand, she flipped through months of notes to November. Let's see . . . why not start with yesterday's entry? Surely her antics on the Cat Gut train warranted at least a page's worth of Elliot's judgment. But, before Rachel could find yesterday's date, the journal fanned open to the bookmark, holding a spot in late October's pages. What did Elliot do in October that he considered so special?

She searched the marked pages expecting to find trivial remarks about homework (as if homework were of any concern to Elliot) or about his after-school hours spent dusting fossilized pots at the SIMA museum with Uncle Mason. She found instead a table of numbers looking more like a math textbook than a diary, and short notations in fancy scripted handwriting. And there were no pictures. Elliot always drew pictures.

Rachel could hardly believe what she read. She tried hard not to believe it, actually. But there it was, in black and white. A neatly drawn table of rows and columns filled with artifacts and figures. Each figure had a dollar sign in front of it, and most had three or more zeros behind:

Two terra cotta water jars,
Northern Israel (one chipped) $25,000
Pharoah Thutmose III figurine,
Dynasty XVIII $350,000
Stone spice mill,
from ancient city of Jericho $12,000
Ostraca (2),
circa 1950 B.C. from Hebron $40,000
Gold earrings, inlaid—Upper Egypt,
circa 1400 B.C $170,000

And on it went. At the bottom were conversions for each price to British pounds.

So . . . that explained the unusual latch on the leather cover and the fancy bookmark. This wasn't Elliot's journal at all. True, Elliot's handwriting matched everything else about him—careful, meticulous, almost perfect. Too perfect as far as she was concerned. But he couldn't write like *this*. No, this journal belonged to someone with even greater attention to detail . . . someone older and wiser. And someone who knew the value of artifacts on the open market. The open *black* market.

"That weasel!" Rachel fumed aloud. She glanced toward the hillside where Elliot knelt digging in the dirt. With angry jerks, she skipped through the journal's open pages. It took a few moments to figure it all out, but when she did, everything crystallized in her snooping mind. A bright, young archeologist travels the world, visiting dozens of fruitful dig sites, providing invaluable expertise. He becomes the darling of the scientific community, riding on the coattails of an older, respected dirt-digger. And all the while he is stealing everyone blind. With each new dig his experience grows, as does his filthy bank account. Rachel had to give Nigel credit . . . it was a smart scam. Had she been ten years older, she might have thought of it herself, and she certainly wouldn't be trading goats for favors. But when she thought of how many good people were tricked, including Uncle Mason and Dr. Cunningham, she began to seethe. Her anger reached the boiling point when she turned the page and found last night's journal entry, dated November 21. Nigel had written:

Plan to travel to Jerusalem tomorrow after dropping off Conner's son and the niece at the nearby moshav. Bright lad, that Elliot—he might just stumble onto something worthwhile. I suppose it will be necessary for the girl to accompany us. Not quite sure why Conner brings her along on these expeditions. She hasn't much to contribute . . . actually, she can be a bit of a twit.

"Twit?" She practically screamed. "So, I'm a twit, am I?" Deep down she knew she could be a twit, when convenient. That was just one side of her colorful personality. But to be called one, in writing no less, was infuriating. Downright hurtful. With hands trembling in anger, she slapped the journal shut. "That's it, then," Rachel vowed. "Nigel Chatsworth, you have just messed with the wrong twit."

She fitted the leather book back into her small travel bag, not yet certain what to do with it. Feeding it to Selah, page by page, might be entertaining. Or perhaps she would bury it, creating another artifact near Lachish. Centuries later, another generation of dirt-diggers would comb through new layers of limestone to find a leather-bound book with a gold latch. And after reading the journal entries, they would conclude that the city had been ruled by Rachel the Twittite.

Or . . . perhaps she would simply keep it. Nigel would miss it, of course, probably become frantic to find it. That seemed the best route to revenge. Besides, his concern over losing it might force him to make a mistake, and when the time was right, Rachel could expose his naughty little plans. She determined to keep the journal a secret . . . for now.

In her anger she failed to notice Elliot's return.

"You okay?" His question startled her.

"Uh . . . yes. Fine." She wiggled her shoulders a little. "So . . . what did you find—a golden calf or something?"

"Nope. Just this." Elliot held up a flattened piece of aluminum with the familiar Pepsi® logo printed across it in unfamiliar Hebrew letters. "I hope we have better luck at the cistern."

CHAPTER 9

"Well? I thought we were traveling to some cave near Dullsville."

"Adullam." Elliot's total concentration lay on the road ahead and the hilly terrain beyond.

She grew impatient, probably as a result of her hurt and anger with Nigel's journal entries.

"We've passed the road to the ruins of Adullam, haven't we? And unless you have driven us to another planet, I would call those holes and hollows up there in the hills 'caves.' Wouldn't you?"

"Uh-huh." He drove steadily on.

"Then stop the stupid Jeep!" she bellowed.

His eyes never left the road.

"I did some reading last night, after our little talk with Aron. Do me a favor. Pull that Bible out of my travel bag, would you? Flip it open to the bookmarked page."

With a loud sigh of annoyance, Rachel did as he asked. She thumbed over to an old envelope holding a spot in the softbound book.

"Now read out loud, everywhere I've put a star in the margin."

Rachel read silently first, and found that this was the story Elliot had talked of earlier. David, the Hebrew shepherd boy who grew up to be King of Israel, battled Goliath the Giant. She skimmed through a description of Goliath, his armor, his weapons, and his ill temper, until she came to Elliot's first star. Then she read aloud.

"'His spear shaft was like a weaver's rod, and its iron point weighed six hundred shekels.'" She looked up for a moment, and her gaze met Elliot's Cheshire-cat grin. "And?" she inquired.

"Six hundred shekels. That figures out to be around six kilograms—roughly fifteen pounds. Keep reading." Elliot grabbed at his hat with one hand as he guided the Jeep along the fading road with the other.

She read ahead through the part where David gathered five stones from the stream bed and challenged the giant while armed with nothing more than a leather sling and stones. Star number two appeared in the margin.

"'As the Philistine moved closer to attack him, David ran quickly toward the battle line to meet him. Reaching into his bag and taking out a stone, he slung it and struck the Philistine on the forehead. The stone sank into his forehead, and he fell facedown on the ground.'" Rachel felt her face screw into a grimace as she read on. "'. . . After he killed him, he cut off his head with the sword.' Well now, that's pleasant, isn't it? I suppose the giant deserved it, though. He was quite rude."

Elliot had slowed the Jeep to a crawl. The road ahead had all but disappeared, just as Jeepers had predicted it would. Surrounding them were hills that suddenly seemed more rugged and foreboding than Rachel expected. A low pillar of darkening clouds rose above the hills along one side, casting an eerie glow of light and shadow across the bony limestone crags and scruffy clumps of vegetation.

"Where are we?"

"Flip over a few pages," answered Elliot, "to the last star." She glared at him but did as he asked.

" 'David left Gath and escaped to the cave of Adullam.'" She tapped the page with her forefinger. "See? The cave, like I told you. That's where Nigel planned to search for treasures, isn't it? And we all know how successful *he* has been." She couldn't stop the sarcasm in her voice.

Elliot killed the Jeep's engine and turned to point over his right shoulder to the south. "That hill back there is the stronghold of David. That's the cave site you just read about. It's still there, three thousand years later. And the valley over there by the satellite dish," he went on, pointing west, "where you rescued the goat and nearly got us all killed on the train? That's where David gathered the stones and felled Goliath." He pulled the keys from the ignition and slipped them into his shirt pocket. "You remember that iron spear point I found in the pantry back at the dig? I weighed it. Guess how much it weighed?"

"Two thousand times more than your brain?" Rachel replied without hesitation.

He smiled. "Close. It weighed fifteen pounds."

"The same as Goliath's spear point."

"Yep." He adjusted his glasses. "About five times heavier than normal. It would take a giant of a man to heave a spear that size. What if . . ." He swallowed hard. "What if that spear point really belonged to Goliath, the giant of Gath? Imagine what other items might be here, and think of what they could teach us about the past."

"Maybe we should be looking in kitchen pantries instead of cisterns and caves," Rachel said softly.

"Makes you wonder how on earth it got there among the skillets, doesn't it? Probably misplaced by local workers months, or even years, ago."

Spearheads in kitchen pantries were no longer a mystery to Rachel. She knew something Elliot didn't know, and she knew why the iron artifact was hidden among the cookware. Nigel Chatsworth, Black Marketeer, had stashed it there. Not years, not months, but hours before Elliot found it. Nigel didn't just happen to show up in the kitchen that morning. He came to retrieve his prize and, although he covered himself well, he was shocked to learn that a twelve-year-old boy had scooped him.

Elliot stepped from the Jeep. He pressed his hat tight to his head and slung his satchel over one shoulder.

"Three thousand years ago, no matter who or where you were, one thing was essential to survival—fresh water. People fought and killed one another for control of a cistern. If my research is correct, the cistern at the end of this road was crucial to the stronghold of

Adullam. If we hope to find anything David and his men left behind, it will be here."

"You sound just like Uncle Mason."

Elliot laughed and pointed to Rachel's borrowed hat. "And you *look* just like an archeologist."

Coming from Elliot, that was quite a compliment. She hid her flicker of pride behind her response. "Oh, really? What a coincidence. You look just like an artifact."

Without another word, Elliot led the way up the hillside east of the dead-end road. They hiked ten minutes or so . . . long enough for Rachel to stub her toe once and scrape her knee twice. She grew hungry, a little tired, thirsty for tea, and more than a little bit cranky. Being an archeologist was fun for a short while. But now it was getting boring.

"Let's find a spot of shade and have a snack," she suggested.

"I'm sure it's close by," Elliot muttered to himself. He kept his pace despite her nagging. Finally he hiked over a rocky bulge jutting from the hillside, then stopped and unshouldered his bag. Rachel caught up to him, ready to plop down and rest. Instead of a shaded plateau, however, she found herself on the rim of a rock cistern nestled into the base of the green Judean hillside. Its opening was circular, more or less, much too wide to jump across, and quite common-looking as far as ancient cisterns were concerned. They had passed several others on the way to Cat Gut yesterday that were smaller but very similar. Below her feet trailed a narrow stone stairway hewn into the side of the open cistern. The steps hugged the inside wall of the cistern in a lazy spiral downward to the rock bottom about five meters below. The autumn breeze blowing across the opening created a low whistling sound—as if someone were blowing gently across the top of a gigantic pop bottle.

Two square openings, positioned opposite one another at the bottom of the cistern, led away from the clouded sunshine and into hidden rooms beyond.

Elliot tipped his hat in her direction and smiled an ivory grin. "This is it—the cistern Aron talked about, north of Adullam. One of them, anyway." He pointed down to the chamber opening on the far side of the cistern. "Let's see where that one leads, shall we?"

They were supposed to be sightseeing in the hills, not circling the innards of what used to be Adullam's sewer system. Then again, if a thunderstorm hit, which looked likely, it might be nice to have a roof over their heads.

Rachel's answer surprised her as much as it appeared to surprise Elliot. "Follow me." She twisted her pack out of the way and descended the stairs.

At the bottom, she cupped her hands to her mouth, guaranteeing a loud voice inside the hollow cistern to call up to the top. "Would you mind ever so much telling me again what we're doing here in this gigantic sinkhole?"

Elliot came down after her and led her through a narrow opening into the side chamber. He immediately pulled a small trip-hammer from his Pony Express bag and hoisted himself up onto a narrow ledge cut partway up the wall. Taking great care, he continued to inch his way along the ledge. With each step he paused to lightly hammer the limestone wall.

"I've got an idea," he answered at last, his eyes scanning the wall surface. "More like a hunch, really."

"I don't need any of your grand ideas, nor your silly hunches." She shadowed his steps, keeping to the floor of the cistern until she came to stand just below him, watching him step and tap like a confused woodpecker. "What I really need is another candy bar." She walked ahead several meters to a point where the ledge widened slightly and sloped downward to form what looked like a limestone bench in one corner of the passageway. There she sat, unzipped her pack, grabbed a candy bar and, with a heavy sigh aimed in Elliot's direction, began to munch away.

Elliot continued to search the wall with his hands and hammer.

"It's bound to be here somewhere," he said, almost to himself. "If you were a king, driven out by enemies into these hills, and this cistern was your closest source of water . . . wouldn't you make sure you had a safe place to go in case of a sneak attack or something?"

"First of all," Rachel began between gooey bites, "I would be a queen, not a king. Secondly, no one foolish enough to be my enemy would dare try to sneak attack *me*. And if I were Queen, I wouldn't be wallowing around in this rock hole. And I would jolly well carry my own canteen for water instead of drinking rain water from this old sewer system."

The hammer tapping stopped momentarily. "This isn't a sewer. It's an aqueduct designed to channel rainwater through natural openings in the stone into holding areas like the one your feet are resting on."

Rachel looked at the cistern floor beneath her shoes and immediately pulled her knees up to her chin, mostly as a gesture to aggravate Elliot. In doing so, she lost her balance and tilted backward against her travel pack behind her. A small grinding sound, like rock against rock, rattled in her ears. For an instant she thought it might be faint thunder from the approaching storm. She bumped backward again, this time on purpose, and again the sound of moving stone answered.

"My guess is that armies had secret chambers scattered throughout cisterns like this one, with hidden openings of some kind," Elliot continued. "Natural little washouts where water has made nooks and crannies. They would be perfect places to hide. I'd expect to find one right about . . ."

"Here," Rachel said simply. She turned and pushed hard against the thin slab of vertical limestone behind her, which opened slowly to reveal a large washout carved into the rock.

He stared at her in amazement. "You found one!"

"Of course I found one. I've grown tired of listening to the annoying tapping sound of that hammer of yours." She peered past the movable slab into the chamber beyond. "I wouldn't exactly call this a cranny." She squinted into the darkened room. "A granddaddy cranny perhaps."

Elliot had clambered down from the ledge to peer

over her shoulder. "Goodness Agnes!" he blurted, followed by a quick adjustment of his glasses. "It's as big as our living room back home!"

Rachel leaned in. "Deeper, I would say." The floor of the hidden chamber laid nearly two meters below the opening. A strong musty smell curled around her face. "Augh! It smells frightful!"

"Probably hasn't been open to fresh air for years. Maybe centuries." Elliot plopped his hiking pack on the limestone bench and fished out a miniature flashlight. As his light surveyed the chamber floor, Rachel saw a smooth sea of stone littered with boulders of all sizes. He turned toward her and shone the light playfully in her eyes. "Okay, Archeology Queen, let's see where it leads." Again Elliot shone the light through the opening, then followed it in, feet first.

Rachel heard his shoes thump against the stone floor. They sounded miles away.

"You are out of your mind!" she answered. Slowly she dangled one leg, then the other, over the lip of the opening into the chamber. Her feet swung freely out into empty space just as a sharp clap of thunder nearly jolted her from the ledge.

"C'mon in," whispered Elliot. He shone the flashlight below her, lighting a landing spot on the floor.

"How do you propose to climb out of this place? Your moth-eaten hat is lower than my feet!"

"Simple. Archeologist Rule Number Ten: Look before you leap. There's a natural stone step carved into the wall just below the ledge. One hop and we're out."

Rachel closed her eyes and threatened, "If I land on a snake you're a dead man." Then she held her pack and its remaining candy bars close to her chest and dropped into the chamber.

CHAPTER 10

Rachel's feet thudded against the hard limestone floor.

"Don't trip on the boulders," Elliot warned. His voice, barely a whisper, resonated inside the hollowed room.

Already Rachel's eyes had grown accustomed to the partial darkness. The opening through which they had come cast a faint shaft of light across the floor, as if painting a path through the boulders. A distant patter of raindrops now tapped outside the chamber's entrance and grew steadily louder with each new clap of thunder. That brewing storm of Uncle Mason's finally had arrived, just as predicted.

"This is exactly what I'd hoped to find," Elliot went on. "If there aren't any artifacts in here, I'll eat my hat."

"Oh really?" Rachel said drolly. "That's a promise, then? Because if it is, I will personally make certain you swallow every disgusting piece of that nasty thing." She strapped her travel bag around her waist and stomped one foot, then the other, against the dense chamber floor. "If there *is* anything hidden under here, you will need a jackhammer to find it."

"Yeah, I see that," he answered. "Stomp your feet again, okay? I want to check something."

Rarely was Rachel asked to stomp her feet, although she had done it plenty of times when she shouldn't have. Happily, she obliged. Elliot stooped to one knee, cocking his head sideways for a better view of the floor beneath them.

"Funny . . . there's no dust. I'd expect a major dust layer to accumulate in a sealed chamber over time." He stood. "So where's the dust?"

"Maybe Goliath and his giant buddies come by and vacuum once a week."

"Or," he continued, ignoring her, "this is one of the washouts that used to hold well water." He squinted upward at the darkness above them. "Mmmm . . ." Next he crossed to one side of the chamber, bent down, and ran a finger along the seam where the floor and the wall met. "Mmmm . . ."

Rachel watched him with growing impatience. "Stop that blasted humming and tell me what you've found!"

"See those small crevices in the rock?" he asked, pointing toward the ceiling.

Rachel looked but saw nothing in the dark ceiling corners.

"Yes," she lied.

"Those used to channel rainwater into the cistern for storage thousands of years ago. Probably still do in fact. But these little cracks that have formed along the wall line allow it to seep out now. I guess the cistern has settled a bit." He tucked his trip-hammer into his shoulder bag as he spoke. "You know, we should bring

Nigel here. He might—"

"We shall do nothing of the sort!" she snorted. The tone of her own voice surprised her. "I mean . . . we've found this place, haven't we? We needn't drag in a den of dirt-diggers just to take it for themselves." She wasn't prepared to tell Elliot the whole story. Not quite yet.

He gave her his typical, trusting response. "Archeologists share information with each other. That's how scientific knowledge moves forward."

That was all the urging she needed. "Well then, let me move you forward with a tidbit of knowledge, Mr. Shared Information. Dr. Nigel Chatsworth, dashing archeologist and kitchen helper, is a sniveling sneak— a crook." She unzipped her travel bag. "You wonder how that spearhead got into the pantry? Nigel put it there. And those treasures stolen from the museum in Jerusalem—do you know where they are? Somewhere in Nigel Chatsworth's drawing room. He's an artifact runner." She clenched her teeth. "A cheat."

"What are you talking about?"

"Here." She handed him Nigel's journal, then folded her arms across her chest. "Open it to October 3."

Fortunately, Elliot was a fast reader, even while juggling a flashlight to read by. As he read, he adjusted his glasses and tugged at his worn hat. Finally, he looked up from the neatly written notes.

"Now check out October 15 and 22," she went on, arms still tightly folded. Elliot scanned the dated pages just as she asked. "Now," she added with an extra push in her voice, "read the November 22 entry."

She waited.

When he had read partway down the page, he glanced up at her. "Twit?"

"Oh, don't bother with the 'twit' part! Just read on!"

Having read the page, he thumbed through several more journal entries and finally closed the book, his thumb resting on its gold latch. "Where did you get this?"

"From Nigel—where did you suppose?"

"*How* did you get this?" he pressed.

"Well now . . . if I told you that you would feel obliged to tell Uncle Mason, then we might both be in for a time of it. I snooped it, if you must know." She failed to mention that she had snooped it by accident, thinking it was Elliot's.

He held out the journal. "Nigel knows you've got this?"

"I don't know. I imagine he knows it's missing by now."

"Goodness Agnes!" he said under his breath. "We've got to tell Dad. And Dr. Cunningham."

Rachel snatched the book from his hands. "Not just yet. I haven't decided how to use this information to our best advantage."

Elliot shone the flashlight straight into her eyes, half blinding her.

"This isn't a game, Rachel. We're not playing tennis here. Nigel may be rummaging through artifacts at the museum as we speak."

"Let him rummage. As long as we have this," she crowed, waving the journal in the air, "we have *him.*"

"It's the artifacts I'm worried about. Once they move into the black market trade, they may never be recovered." He paused for a moment. "Maybe we should leave now—go back to Lachish and warn Dad."

"Oh . . . I suppose you're right. As usual." With a heavy sigh she zipped the journal into her pack. "Come on then."

"Uh, one small problem," Elliot said sheepishly.

"What is it now?" she retorted, already dreading the jaunt back to the farm in a roofless Jeep—in the rain.

"I'm stuck." He turned the flashlight downward onto the floor, where his left foot was wedged between two beachball-sized boulders. Then he flashed the light onto his own grinning face. "Honest."

"How . . . I won't even ask!" Rachel hissed. "What do you expect me to do?"

"Push." He shone the light across one boulder. "Help me shove this thing to one side."

He pocketed the flashlight and together the two strained against the unmoving mass of stone. Nothing happened. Obviously the big boulder hadn't been moved for centuries and had no intention of moving now.

Elliot drew a deep breath and surveyed the chamber through squinted eyes. Then he handed her the flashlight. "Guess it's a little heavier than it looks. See if you can find a flat rock to pry with. I need something to wedge between my foot and one of the boulders to free it up."

Rachel chuckled softly, more for Elliot's benefit than for her own.

"First I arrange transportation for this little expedition of yours by trading my goat for a dying Jeep. And now I'm expected to create a tool to prevent your foot from becoming an artifact. You're quite fortunate I bothered to offer my presence today, are you not?"

Slowly she circled the chamber, the flashlight beam bouncing along its curving walls. Flat rocks were a rare commodity in this cistern—she hadn't recalled seeing anything flat, in fact. Everything was smooth and rounded. However, as she swept the light across the upper portion of one wall, a small, oval shadow appeared. She extended her arm and marched to the wall for a closer look.

"How odd," she muttered. She looked back over her shoulder at Elliot. "There's a small flat rock stuck to the wall."

"Great. Toss it down."

"This dark room seems to have affected your hearing . . . I said it is *stuck to the wall!*" Fitting her feet into a short series of hewn stone insets, Rachel climbed a meter or so up the wall and groped for the rock. She leaned closer for a better look, only to discover a series of holes, deep holes, twice the size of her arm, gouged into the wall beside the flat rock. She also noticed that the rock was held in place by a gooey-looking substance.

"The Flinstones who came here—they didn't happen to invent silly putty, did they?" Rachel asked. "Because this flat stone seems to be hung here with old peanut butter or something. The nasty stuff is blobbed all around these enormous woodpecker holes in the rock as well!"

"Holes?"

"Yes, holes. Deep enough to . . ." A terrifying thought struck her. "These are snake holes, aren't they! Just big enough for some long, slinky snake to sleep in! I warned you . . . if . . ."

"Dugouts," Elliot grunted. He was pushing with all of his might against the boulder. "Perfect places to stash things where enemies couldn't find them. Like weapons and jewelry." He stopped to let out a sigh. "And the 'peanut butter' is probably resin used to seal the dugouts from water. I told you we'd find artifacts in here. Just pull down the rock so I can get my foot back, okay?"

Rachel laid the flashlight aside and gave a grunt of her own as she twisted her hands against the flat stone. Slowly it loosened, finally yielding to her grasp with a hollow *pop!* Another of Elliot's dugouts lay beneath it.

"Hello," she said. "What's this?" The flashlight's beam lit the long, narrow hole before her. Within the hole rested a solid pole of some sort.

"Will a pipe do?" she asked. "To pry your foot loose, I mean?"

"A pipe?"

"Well, I believe that's what it is." Carefully she wrapped her fingers around the pole and, to her surprise, it felt as though she had grabbed a tree branch. She drew the item from its resting place and discovered it was much longer than she had first assumed. Two meters long, or more.

"It's . . . it's wood," she announced. The smooth shaft

turned slowly in her hand. "Almost like a walking stick, or a cane, perhaps."

"Wood?" came Elliot's shocked reply. "I'd better have a look at that."

"You had better use the blasted thing to free that foot of yours first. I do not intend to stand here in the dark while you analyze a tree branch."

Rachel retraced her steps down the wall and dropped to the floor. Suddenly she froze. Something was winding its way around the front of her hiking shoes . . . slowly, silently, deliberately. It felt cool and constant and soon had worked its way to her heel. Too frightened to look down, she tried instead to scream, but no sound would leave her throat. Visions of dugout snakes the size of fire hoses pulsed in her brain. Time stood still.

"Rachel? The stick? In this lifetime? My foot's stuck, remember?"

A coarse whisper, sounding barely human, slipped from her mouth. "Elliot! There is something . . . crawling . . . on . . . my foot."

"The flashlight! Shine the flashlight down there!"

Her brain directed her wrist to turn in slow motion toward the floor, not really wanting to see what might be slithering there. A beam of light reflected from the wet surface back into her eyes. Then Elliot's voice reached her ears.

"Water. It's a puddle of rainwater."

Rachel felt her shoulders collapse in one giant sigh of relief. The feathery sound of water misting into the chamber reassured her.

"Oh, I thought it was a snake! I thought I was doomed. I thought—"

"We might have been better off if it *were* a snake," Elliot said with a certain sense of urgency.

Irritated, she poked at him with the stick. "Whatever are you saying?"

"This is a cistern," he said as he grabbed the wooden shaft. "A leaky one, maybe, but it's still a cistern. It's made to channel and store water in these chambers. Which means it may get deep in here very quickly." He began to squirm and pry at his trapped foot with the stick. "Which means I better get loose," he grunted, "or sprout gills."

Already Rachel felt the dampness seeping across the tops of her shoes. Elliot's nervousness gave her the jitters.

"What shall I do?"

"Push against the stick, hard!" he called out. The mist of water had become a steady trickle now, and dozens of separate miniature waterfalls appeared from the openings along the chamber ceiling. Together they pushed and pulled. Elliot shifted his weight on the stick and twisted, first toward his body then away. No luck. His foot wouldn't budge. Minutes went by. The rush of water grew slightly louder. Finally Rachel's exasperated cousin squeezed her wrist.

"I think it's time you went for help," he said. Rachel felt the tension in his usually calm voice.

"Help? Where? Who?"

"Here," he called out over the hollow splashes around them, "take the Jeep." He fished the keys from his shirt pocket and held them out to her. In her haste to grab the shiny metal ring from his fist, she fumbled the keys into the rising water at her feet.

"Blast!" she cried out in desperation.

"Don't move! Just squat where you are and feel for the keys under the water!"

She did as Elliot instructed. The rainwater was much colder to the touch than her shoes and socks had revealed. And slimy. Her hands felt cold and slippery all at the same time. She fanned out her fingers and raked them back and forth along the hard floor of the chamber.

"I can't see anything!"

"They've got to be there, Rachel. Keep searching."

Her knees dipped forward into the water as she moved her arms in wide circles to sweep the floor. Several small boulders grazed her knuckles. Already the water had risen enough to dampen her wrists. Suddenly her thumb rapped against something heavy and metallic. Instinctively she latched on.

"I've got them!"

"You've got to find help. Drive back toward the ruins at Adullam and find someone—anyone. Get Aron if you have to. Just go!"

She stuffed the keys in her pack. Then she felt her heart sink. "I'm not certain I can drive the Jeep."

"You can drive the Jeep. Just pat your head and rub your stomach, remember? Go! Now!"

Rachel, panicked, sloshed back across the chamber floor toward the only real opening in the room, the one they had entered minutes earlier, which now lay nearly three feet above her. Already the water had covered her toes and it showed no signs of slowing. *If only the opening were closer to the floor,* she thought. *The water would spill out before it gets too deep.* When she reached the far wall, she groped into the half-darkness for the ledge Elliot promised. Finally her fingers found its rough edge, and with a single fear-powered hop, Rachel tumbled up and out through the chamber's rectangular hole. The steady sound of rainwater channeling its way into the cistern reminded her of the horrible reality: by the time the water reached the opening, Elliot would be trapped under half a meter of water.

"Rachel."

She turned to face Elliot.

"Yes?"

"Do me a favor. Hurry, would you?" He lifted his dig-site hat, dragged a hand across his sweaty hair, then snugged the hat back on his head. He cracked a weak half-smile. "I'd hate for my hat to get wet."

Rachel bounded to the spiral stone staircase and mounted it, two steps at a time. Still, it seemed to take forever to climb. She didn't even notice the steady pelting of rain on her face until she reached the top step. In the distance sat Jeepers' Jeep—its wet, rusty frame instantly became a hulking metal monster, daring her to conquer it. And yet it beckoned to her as the only friend she had that could save Elliot.

The gentle whistle of breeze slipping over the open cistern was gone. An odd, peaceful sound, like that of a babbling brook or a distant mountain stream, now rose from below her. But as she raced toward the Jeep, the peaceful stream became an echoing splash of fast-falling water, drowning out all other sounds, and trying to drown her cousin as well.

Suddenly Rachel felt alone. Very alone.

CHAPTER 11

"Okay, okay . . ." Rachel whispered to herself. "I can do this." She fumbled the Jeep keys into the ignition. "Right. Keys are in, I start the Jeep, I drive to . . ." She looked ahead through the rain, only to realize the road ended at the Jeep tires. "I back the Jeep *up*, then I drive toward the ruins at Dullsville for help. After all, there *is* only one road . . . isn't there?" The long silence that followed told her she had grown terribly unsure of herself.

An army of goosebumps found its way up and down her arms, which had been chilled by the storm front's steady rain. The sloping bluffs surrounding her seemed bigger and less friendly than they had an hour earlier. They now felt close and pressing, causing her to breathe in quick, sharp breaths. A small bead of rainwater collected on her hat brim, flowed to the rear, and trickled down her back in a cold, constant drip—a startling reminder of how quickly the cistern might fill with water. Somehow she collected her wits and twisted the key in her wet hand.

"All right then, Jeep. It's me and you against the rain. Let's gooo . . . "

Wham! The Jeep jolted forward with such force that Rachel's hand flew from the steering wheel. Instantly, she jerked around to see what had struck her from behind. There was nothing there but gray skies and pouring rain. *Of course! The clutch.* She had forgotten to press down the clutch when she turned the key! With her jittering left leg she slammed the clutch pedal to the floor and again twisted the ignition key. This time the engine popped over, then settled into a ragged hum. Next she searched the numbers and letters on the gearshift knob until she found the position for "R"—"reverse." With a shove on the stick shift the Jeep clunked into backing gear. She felt a sigh escape from her lips.

"Rub my stomach, pat my head. Rub my stomach, pat my head. That's what Elliot said. Or was it rub my head, pat my stomach? Blast! Why can't they build these stupid things to drive themselves, without needing four arms and ten legs!"

Slowly, Rachel pushed the gas pedal with her right foot. The engine raced but the Jeep stood dead still. "Now I simply let out on the clutch pedal, just like Elliot did . . . "

Wham! The Jeep jolted again, backward this time, with such force that her hat tumbled into the puddle of rainwater and goat hair soaking the backseat. The engine fell absolutely silent. Another quick turn of the key and the engine hummed again. This time she eased off the clutch rather than popping it from the floorboard. The vehicle backed and turned in the direction she guided it. In moments she had reversed her direction and pointed the Jeep toward Lachish.

She gathered her thoughts, retrieved her hat, and, with a hard push forward on the stick shift, she forced the Jeep into first gear. The clutch pedal eased beneath her left foot, the Jeep shuddered, then lurched forward and rolled on its own. A wave of relief swept over her.

"Well now, that's not so bad, is it?" she said aloud. With a slight urging from her right foot, the engine revved up a notch. A breath of wet air funneled through the opening where the windshield should have been. Slowly, the rough-riding rust pile gained speed. As the tires turned against the muddy pathway, however, the engine whined and refused to go faster.

"Come on, come on!"

Shift! It was time to shift gears again. Just for practice, Rachel patted her head and rubbed her stomach. She pulled the stick toward her, just as she had seen Elliot do. A terrible grinding sound, like fingernails on a chalkboard, wrenched beneath her feet.

"Blast!"

A quick stomp on the clutch allowed the gearshift to slip easily into second gear. Her speed picked up again. Only then did she realize that her hat, her clothes, and the entire interior of the Jeep had swelled fat and soggy with rain. Tucking her hat brim against the driving rainstorm, Rachel pressed on.

"At least this absurd hat isn't completely worthless!" she yelled into the rain. Her own voice now became her only encouragement—very much like her childhood in Europe, actually—where a great deal of time was spent alone, or with nannies hired to keep her out of trouble. An impossible task, Rachel admitted. She had been in this situation dozens of times before—not driving a pesky Jeep through roadless limestone hills in an Israeli thunderstorm, of course—but alone and worried with no one to rely on but herself. And her wits.

"You can't win, you know!" she burst aloud, her fist rising under its own willpower to confront the rain. "Oh, you can try! You can swallow me up if you like, but you can't win! I've got years of practice on you. I've survived nannies and London fog and Mother's ridiculous schedules, and . . . and even Elliot Conner. You are no match for Rachel Ashton!"

The gray sky answered with a muffled roll of thunder. In one fluid motion, she threw the stick shift forward while stomping on the clutch. The Jeep smoothly found third gear. Rachel could almost gauge her speed now by the force of raindrops against her shirt. Before she knew it she had reached the main road. But the occasional traveler or donkey, so familiar on the sunny countryside trip to Cat Gut a day earlier, were absent. She met only rain.

She tried to preoccupy her brain with pleasant thoughts—like the tongue-lashing she would give Elliot for making her wallow in this storm to save his hide. Or the satisfaction she would feel when returning Nigel Chatsworth's journal to him in front of Dr. Cunningham and Uncle Mason. "I believe you dropped this," she would say. "And 'the Twit' found it." Black market indeed! She couldn't fathom why anyone would pay such outrageous prices for pieces of clay and metal dug from some hillside hole. Then again, she had spent enough time around Uncle Mason and Elliot to gain an appreciation for their world of digs and dead people. Funny how that feeling had grown strong and unbreakable in the past few minutes. All that really mattered now was freeing Elliot before *he* became ancient history.

A second rush of hope suddenly pulsed within her. "I'll reach help in time. It isn't that much farther and the rain has let up a bit. And even if I don't find help soon, he'll make it," she said of Elliot. "He always manages. He's a slippery one. . . ." A weak half-smile tightened her cheeks. "Although not quite as slippery as me."

She now focused her thoughts on the rain, trying to make it stop. Wet clothes and brisk air had begun to numb her skin. The chill forced its way deeper into her bones, but she refused to allow it in. Up ahead, two long white buildings appeared through the mist. If she strained, Rachel could almost hear the gobble of turkeys. Two shadowy figures floated near the road on the north side of the *moshav*, one tall, the other short and squatty. Rachel switched on the Jeep headlights. The dull shine of two round goat eyes and a glint of gold tooth flashed through the beams.

"Jeepers!"

The taller figure stepped into the rain from beneath a small lean-to in the turkey yard. Aron Segal and his gold tooth waved the Jeep to an abrupt stop. Rachel killed the engine and hopped from the driver's seat into the wetter passenger side.

"Please!" she panted. "Elliot is in trouble! You must come quickly!"

Jeepers pulled his head covering tighter to his neck to slow the rain from wetting him through. His gold tooth disappeared into his mustache.

"What is it?"

"Elliot! He is trapped in a cistern! Near the caves! We found a secret passageway, but the rainwater began to leak into . . ."

Before she could finish, Jeepers popped open the Jeep door, climbed behind the wheel, cranked the engine, and forced the Jeep into a tight U-turn, which brought its headlights face-to-face with Selah's dull eyes and matted coat of wet, smelly goat hair blocking the road.

Bleeaahhh!

Rachel half-stood in her seat. "Move, you bleating bag of candy bars! Why must you always stand in front of moving vehicles!" Without warning, the small animal launched itself over the side and into the rear seat. And as Jeepers steered them away from the *moshav*, she sputtered under her breath, "We don't need goats! We need something useful . . . like *time*."

Uneven ruts in the weathered road had now become potholes under the attacking rain. With every turn came another bump. Rachel began to feel sorry for herself—nearly as sorry as she felt for Elliot.

"I should be curled by the fireplace in Kentucky right now, reading a good book," she mumbled. "Not jarring across the middle of nowhere in a Jeep. In the rain.

With a goat!" she practically yelled.

Jeepers didn't respond, nor did she expect him to. But he would have to listen anyway.

" 'Let's go in the cistern,' he says! Right! It's preparing to rain and he wants to look for old pots in a cistern. Then there we are driving a Jeep—alone—and I'm thinking, 'Oh, how adventurous!' *How stupid.* I'd be better off taking my chances with Mother. At least she doesn't wear dirty old dig hats."

Rachel swiped her forearm at the trickle of raindrops streaming down her face. Yet another dip in the muddied road bounced her and Selah in their seats with a pounding jolt.

"And what's more," she went on, squeezing her hat against her head for fear of losing it in the wild ride, "we've Nigel Chatsworth to reckon with now."

"The archeologist who drove you to the *moshav*?" her driver finally spoke up.

"Yes! He's a snake! A fraud and a cheat! And together, Elliot and I can prove it."

"I thought you knew he was a thief."

Rachel twisted to face Jeepers, shielding her eyes from the rain.

"And just how was I supposed to know *that*? He seemed to be a fine chap, quite impressive. He even fooled Elliot. And Uncle Mason."

"He bears what we call 'the mark of a fortunate thief.'" Tiny droplets of rain beaded on the surface of Jeeper's mustache.

Rachel felt her eyes squint. The image of Nigel Chatsworth turned over and over in her mind.

Truthquest

"You mean that scar . . . on his wrist?"

Jeepers nodded, rain dripping down his prominent nose with each bob of his head. "I have seen such scars before. Removing the hand of a thief is a fitting punishment in some cultures surrounding us. It discourages the thief from stealing again."

"You mean they just chop it off? How disgusting!"

"The fortunate ones, like your archeologist, escape."

The Jeep rocked suddenly at a large mudhole, prompting Rachel to grab her seat with both hands. She felt lucky to *have* both hands after Jeepers' little enlightening story. Not that she had ever stolen anything, really—borrowed a few things, perhaps . . . and snooped into other people's business a great deal, stretched the truth a bit—but theft had never been high on her priority list.

"How much farther is it?" asked Jeepers.

"Cross the main highway, pass the hill and rubble around Dullsville, then drive on to where the road nearly ends!" she called out through the steady rain. "The cistern is over at the edge of the hillsides, just . . ."

"I know the cistern." His foot grew heavy on the gas pedal—a clear signal to Rachel that Elliot was in far greater danger than she had allowed herself to believe.

After crossing the main road, Jeepers traveled on past the ruins at Adullam and seemed to watch the caves carefully, as if using them for guidance, like a sailor using stars for navigation. The road narrowed a bit. The rain let up slightly. All the while Selah laid behind her, wedged into the small floorboard space in the backseat.

Jeepers brought the Jeep to an abrupt stop.

"Yes, yes!" Rachel realized. "I believe this is it!"

Aron left the Jeep in a rush, before she could swing open her door. The short tails of his old waistcoat flew behind him. Every few steps his shoes sent up miniature splashes as he trotted through small puddles of water collected along the hillside terrain. The pounding of raindrops had given way to a quiet sprinkle—deceivingly calm and relaxing, reminding Rachel of her younger days in Great Britain. But when she finally caught up to Jeepers, standing at the edge of the open cistern, she lost those feelings of serenity. Instead she felt numb and light-headed.

Below them laid the blunt reality of this hilly land and the people who had conquered it thousands of years ago. Despite time and weather, the cistern still worked extremely well. It still guided tiny trickles of rainwater from the hill country into larger trickles that soon became shallow creeks, all winding their way to the cistern like dozens of underground arteries coursing to a pounding heart. To King David and the Philistine giants, the cistern meant life—a way of storing precious water for their survival. But looking down at the lazy swirl of water rising halfway up the cistern's rock steps, Rachel didn't think about life or survival. Instead, her jumbled mind brought only one thought—the memory of what she had told Elliot just days ago: *Why don't you go do something useful? Like drown.*

"The chamber you entered," Jeepers broke through her thoughts, " . . . where is it?"

Rachel stared blankly at the water's surface. "There,

at the bottom of the cistern." Her voice was scarcely more than a whisper.

The chamber, the opening, the boulders, and the bottom of the cistern steps all laid silent and hidden below at least a meter of water. A hand on the back of her wet shirt suddenly brought her back to her senses. It belonged to Jeepers. He was pulling her away from the rocky stairs leading down into the cistern. Rachel had started down them, into the water, without realizing it. Then a dark circle caught her eye. Slowly it bobbed up and down, nudging the stony wall opposite the stairs. Rachel swept the beaded rain from her brow and squinted for a better view. A chill, deeper and stronger than that of her wet clothes in the breeze, crawled under her skin into her bones. She closed her eyes but the image of the dark circle wouldn't go away.

Jeepers came to stand behind her shoulder. "What is that . . . floating in the cistern?"

Rachel covered her closed eyes with her hands.

"Elliot's hat."

CHAPTER 12

"Maybe he found another way out of the cistern," Aron said, trying to console her. He didn't sound too convincing.

"There *was* no other way out!" Rachel barked back. "I was in there, remember? We barely found our way in!" The rush of hope that had sustained her throughout the Jeep ride was all but gone. "What a stupid business, this archeology rot! Grown men like Uncle Mason charging around the world to dig up grass and search for old bricks and pots . . ." She turned to vent her anger and frustration on Jeepers before her guilt overcame her. Less than an hour ago she had begun to feel like an archeologist herself and had even taken pride in the thought. "Is this all it comes to then? Leaky cisterns, black marketeers . . . and turkey farmers?" Instantly, despite her fear and sadness, she wished she could take back her words. In fact, she wished she could take back every cross word she had ever said, especially to Elliot.

Aron Segal's expression remained changeless, as

though he hadn't heard her lump turkey farmers into the same shameful category as black marketeers. Instead, his eyes welled with a compassion Rachel could almost touch. She reached out and grasped the sleeve of his waistcoat.

"Oh . . . Jeepers . . . what shall I tell Uncle Mason?"

His gaze slowly left hers to focus on a shadow approaching from behind, cast by the first rays of sunshine ushering out the storm. Then his gold tooth suddenly appeared.

"Tell him we've found some amazing things!" came the voice at Rachel's back.

She spun around to find her bespectacled cousin—pants soaked from the knees down, and shoes brown with limestone mud—standing in fine form and drier than the both of them.

"But you . . . the water was . . . and your hat . . ." Rachel felt frozen in place by a flood of emotions: shock, surprise, joy, relief—and anger. She had been extremely upset over nearly losing Elliot. Now that he had returned from the dead unannounced, she found herself more upset with *him* for causing her to believe he was dead in the first place. She couldn't even stammer out a response.

Jeepers needed no response. He grasped Elliot's shoulders warmly with both hands and tousled his hair, then ended his greeting with a hug and several pats on the back.

Elliot stepped back and adjusted his glasses.

"You didn't think I'd drowned, did you?" he said to Rachel. "Sorry . . . no such luck. I managed to work my leg free with this 'stick' of yours right after you left, actually." He pumped the stick up and down above his head as if preparing to throw a javelin. Or a spear. "In fact," he continued, "if it weren't for this stick, I'd be wishing for gills about now." He stared for a moment into the swirling water below them. Then, beaming ear to ear, he stood the stick on its end.

Rachel stared at it numbly. She couldn't shake the mixture of feelings she had toward her cousin. She didn't know whether to hug him or hit him. Neither he nor the stick seemed quite real at the moment.

"This is a very special shaft of wood—you might even call it a *giant* discovery in the field of archeology," he finished, still smiling.

Unlike Elliot, Rachel didn't feel like smiling. She felt like a drowned rat in her sopping wet clothes. She was cold and tired and still shaken by her whirlwind Jeep trip. Her emotional tug-of-war between relief and anger over Elliot finally pulled free. Anger won.

"Don't flatter yourself," she sputtered out. "The only worthwhile thing about that stick, which *I* found by the way, is that it saved your sorry life."

The smile quickly faded from his face. "You're right, Rachel. I'd still be down there under my hat if you had-n't been here." He turned toward Jeepers. "She did save my life."

Jeepers raised his eyebrows and nodded slowly.

"Thank you, Rachel," Elliot said. As always, he sounded absolutely sincere. "I should have thanked you sooner. I guess I just got caught up in all the excitement."

She wasn't ready to let him off the hook. How could he have such a casual attitude toward having almost drowned?

"Excitement? Oh, yes, of course. There you are . . . drowning in a cistern while the cousin who saves your neck nearly catches pneumonia driving through monsoon rains, flirting with death at every bumpy turn. I can see how all that excitement might make you forget the little people like me. I mean, all I did was keep you alive." She cleared her throat. "And nearly killed myself doing it," she mumbled just loud enough for both Elliot and Jeepers to hear.

Bleeaahhh!

Selah had joined Elliot and now stood at his side, nibbling at his wet pant leg.

"Make that *two* sorry lives I've saved this week!" Rachel exclaimed. "Both of them Goat Brains!"

The pesky goat nudged at Elliot's wooden stick. In the clearing sunlight it looked much different than it had looked inside the dark cistern. It spanned more than two meters in length. The wood was rich and smooth, and it laid in Elliot's hands like an oversized broom handle. Near one end hung a rusty metal ring, big enough for Rachel to slip her hand through. Just below the ring a series of pictures and designs decorated the wooden pole in a spiral pattern leading down toward the rounded tip. Intricate carvings of diamonds and checkerboards caught Rachel's eye, an, mixed in among the bold shapes were elegantly carved images of birds with curving necks and *S*-shaped bodies.

"What do you make of this?" Elliot handed the mustached turkey-farmer the stick.

Jeepers turned the wooden pole around and around in his hands. Each carved portion received a critical inspection from his fingers. Then he gave his answer. "I have seen no other like it."

Elliot flashed an ivory grin in Rachel's direction. "There *isn't* another stick like it . . . never has been. This is a spear shaft from the late Bronze Age. See that metal ring near the tip? It's modeled after the weaver's rods used to make clothing. The warrior tied a leather strap to it and threw the spear like a javelin." He pointed to an area of worn wood just beyond the rusty ring. "That's where the spear point attached. I'd say this shaft is made to hold . . . oh . . . about fifteen pounds worth of spear point, give or take a pound. Does fifteen pounds sound like a familiar number?"

"Only if you are referring to the amount of water still sloshing around between your ears," Rachel answered.

Elliot chuckled away her rude answer. He was unsinkable—worse yet, his excitement was contagious. This was why she could never stay angry with him for too long. After heaving a deep sigh to show her surrender to his high spirits, she caved in and gave him the answer he wanted.

"You think that spear belonged to the big Goldfish, don't you?"

"I'm sure of it. This is the spear of Goliath the Giant—the same giant David killed with his sling. Remember that spear point in the pantry?"

"The one Nigel Chatsworth squirreled away?"

"Right. I'll bet anything that it fits this like a glove."

He shook his hatless head. "And there's more," he guaranteed. "When I was climbing from the chamber I noticed something—up in the washout space above the opening. It took several tries, but I finally managed to climb up the wall and grab it."

"You climbed around the walls of that chamber as it rushed full of water?" Rachel howled. "Your brain is even smaller than I suspected!"

He unzipped his shoulder bag and fished inside. "It's a Philistine storage jar of some sort. See? You can tell by the style of the face on the lid." He handed the rounded vessel to her. It was small, gold and pot-shaped with an almost cartoon-like face for a lid. Large ears protruded like wings on either side of the broad cheeks and pointed nose. The word "blowfish" popped into Rachel's mind.

"Maybe *you* can tell it belonged to the Flintstones. To me, it's just another ugly face." She glanced again at the thing in her hands. "How disgusting! I can't believe you nearly drowned for this!"

"But it's solid gold! And it's in museum condition!"

"It's hideous, that's what it is!" The dull look in the image's eyes gave her a spooky feeling inside. She shoved it back into Elliot's waiting grasp. Then she noticed an uncomfortable stickiness on her fingers. One look revealed a thin amber substance ringing her fingertips. "Yuk! What *is* this?"

"Resin of some kind. The vessel was sealed with it. Waterproofed. Good thing, too. I imagine this old pot has seen its share of well water." He thumped the lid. "Well . . . aren't you going to ask what was inside?"

"I have no desire to see what a face like that one puts in its belly." She wasn't ready to warm up to Elliot completely. Not yet.

Jeepers huddled closer, still cradling the spear shaft in his fists. "What was in the vessel?"

"Dust . . . and this." Elliot again reached into his satchel. But just as he was revealing his surprise, the groan of an engine topped a hill in the distance. With the groan came the rattling of an old supply truck, its canvas cover swaying with each pothole in its path.

"Nigel!" exclaimed Rachel.

"We can't let him see what we've found," warned Elliot, already running down the hillside. "These artifacts belong in a museum—not in some black market trophy room."

"But why is he coming here?" Rachel yelled after him. "He's supposed to be at the museum."

"He probably sold another artifact, and when he tried to record his sale he found his journal was missing. I'll give you three guesses who he's looking for, and the first two don't count."

Jeepers followed them down to the drying Jeep and motioned them inside. "I know of another road. It will take us back to the *moshav*."

Elliot gathered Selah into his arms and hoisted him into the rear seat. Rachel unstrapped her hiking pack, tossed it in, and quickly followed. In a flash Jeepers cranked the engine, turned the wheel, and sped away from the cistern. But Nigel had already spotted them. The supply truck changed direction, and its engine revved in hot pursuit.

For several minutes they bumped along through short stretches of flat lowland between the sloped hills. Jeepers skillfully shunted the Jeep around boulders and jutting limestone humps scattered along the abandoned road. It was clear, however, that Nigel was no newcomer to the landscape. His supply truck loomed at every turn, each time a little closer.

Rachel rode out the bumps by clinging to the back of Jeepers' seat with one hand and to Elliot with the other. Her grip on his shirt tightened with each bump, and she thought again of how foolish and dangerous this business had become.

"It wasn't fair of you to do that," Rachel called out between bumps.

"Do what?"

"To be dead for awhile . . . I mean, to make us *think* you were dead."

"Believe me, Rachel, getting stuck in a flooded cistern is the last thing I wanted to do." A long silence hung between them. Then an almost invisible smile crept onto Elliot's face. "But . . . when you thought I was dead . . . did you miss me?"

She threw him a glaring squint.

"No," she lied. "But I did miss that ugly hat of yours."

"Goodness Agnes! My hat!" he yelled, grabbing his scalp. "I left it at the cistern!"

"Finally! Something good has come out of this after all."

"But it's my lucky hat!"

"Yes, right. I feel quite lucky at the moment, don't you?" she sneered. "Of course there *is* that small matter of a black marketeer breathing down our necks, probably bent on doing us in . . . otherwise, I feel quite lucky indeed."

The squeak of brakes abruptly ended their conversation. Jeepers angled the Jeep into the corner of a field surrounded by a low stone fence. Within the fence stretched an orchard that followed the curved slope of hillside it occupied. Each tree in the orchard bowed and swayed its collection of low branches gently in the light breeze. Rachel knew Jeepers would not have stopped unless forced to—which meant Nigel had cut them off and left no options. Suddenly the chill of Rachel's damp clothes sent a shiver up her spine—at least she *thought* the shiver was from her damp clothes.

"You should wait here in the orchard," Jeepers said. "I will return for you when it is safe."

"Return?" Rachel questioned. "What do you mean? You can't just dump us here and leave."

The rattling supply truck suddenly crested a low slope less than a hundred meters in front of them.

"Let's go, Rachel," Elliot said sternly.

"This is your fault, Mr. Lucky Moth-eaten Hat!"

Rachel exited the Jeep on one side, careful to tuck Nigel's journal under her arm. Elliot pulled something from his Pony Express bag, then slipped out the other. Together they scampered over the stone fence to lose themselves among the trees. But the sound of the supply truck bore down on them, its thumping tires growling ever closer. Following Elliot's lead, Rachel squatted low to the ground and slunk past several rows of trees.

At this angle they would be difficult to spot unless . . . unless Nigel came searching for them.

A waving hand suddenly caught her attention. It lay at the end of Elliot's athletic arm.

"Split up!" he cried in his loudest whisper. He dropped to all fours and crawled toward a nearby, low-branching tree. Faced with no other choice, she followed his command until she, too, found the hiding shade of a tree with thick foliage. Then she waited. When he finally turned her way, she shrugged at him and mouthed, "Now what?"

His finger pointed straight up, and she read the soundless reply on his lips:

"Climb!"

CHAPTER 13

There, in the middle of the Judean orchard, Rachel's thoughts raced back to her childhood in Great Britain. She never had been the sporting type—oh certainly, she had played soccer now and again—but most events of speed and skill escaped her. Climbing trees, however, did not. Indeed, tree climbing had become second nature at a young age when she discovered it was a marvelous way of hiding from Mother.

Placing one foot against the base of the tree, she grasped the lowest branch with her left hand and effortlessly propelled herself into the first trunk fork. Two more quick moves and her heel found a secure resting place among the higher branches. One final tug up with her arms carried her into a comfortable hiding spot camouflaged all around by leaves nearly four meters off the ground. From here she had a great view of Jeepers, of the arriving supply truck, and even of Elliot struggling with a contrary tree branch. At last he managed to swing a foot into place to occupy a spot level with her own three trees away. She saw his eyes scanning the ground, apparently expecting to find her there.

"Pssst!" she hissed for his attention.

His look of shocked surprise at seeing her high in the tree gave Rachel a great deal of satisfaction. So what if Nigel dragged them away to be sold as slaves on the black market? She had outclimbed Elliot, and he knew it.

"Ho, there!" Nigel's voice called out. Even from this distance, Rachel detected the falseness of his jovial greeting and forced smile. He leaned through the open driver's window to address Jeepers. "I've been trying to catch up to you since the caves." His head nodded toward Adullam. Then he hopped from the supply truck into Jeepers' path. Jeepers had no choice but to confront him.

Rachel watched the two men from her bird's-eye perch, where she had a clear view of Nigel but could now see only Jeepers' back. As Nigel approached the turkey farmer, their voices grew lower and difficult to make out. He appeared to be asking Jeepers a lot of questions that were answered with shrugs and shakes of the head. Finally, Jeepers raised one arm and pointed toward the hillsides, to nowhere in particular.

He's asking about us, she told herself.

Nigel, still talking, walked slowly past their friend to the Jeep. A horrid jolt suddenly pulsed through her body. Their hiking packs lay open in the backseat. How foolish of them! She glanced at Elliot three trees away. His face confirmed her fear that Nigel would see the packs and realize they were hiding nearby, *with* the journal.

" . . . I'm quite certain it is here somewhere," Nigel was saying. Rachel could make out the voices now. "Probably gathered it up with their things by mistake in their rush to go exploring." This was babbling small talk, Rachel knew, to distract Jeepers while scanning about for the book. She could tell by his voice that Nigel didn't believe a word of his own story. Which meant he knew his journal had been stolen, and he had come after the thief as well as the book.

Jeepers jostled Selah, splayed out across the Jeep's backseat like a sphinx, in a lame attempt to cover the hiking packs. But he was too late.

"I believe they have taken everything. . . ." Jeepers began.

"Everything but their hiking packs. Curious." Nigel fumbled his arm inside Rachel's pack until his hand emerged with a half-eaten candy bar, which he threw to the ground with impatience. He lifted the pack out, only to spy Elliot's satchel beneath it. The ugly gold pot bulged from it like a shiny bubble. Scooping the vessel up in his hand, he held it skyward.

"Magnificent! Philistine craftsmanship. These children are quite the artifact hunters, aren't they?" he said almost to himself. Quickly he tucked the pot back into the bag and threw it over his shoulder. "Any other hidden treasures in this old Jeep of yours?" In his rush to find out, Nigel elbowed Selah to one side.

Bleeaahhh!

"Right you are, you smelly creature. Be a good goat

and hop out of the way, won't you?" His prodding hands forced Selah over the spare tire mounted on the Jeep's rear, and onto the wet ground. As the goat hopped away, Nigel's eyes fell on the ancient giant's spear shaft poking from the far side of the Jeep.

"Oh, my! What have we here?" he said slowly. He hoisted the wooden spear in amazement. His hands ran up and down the shaft as if holding delicate glass. When his fingers reached the metal ring, he started. Carefully he traced his finger around and around inside the ring. Then he set the shaft in his open hands, testing it for weight and strength. All the while his head nodded in obvious recognition, as though he had found exactly what he had expected to find. "The shaft . . . of Goliath. It is even more marvelous than I imagined!"

Then, turning to Jeepers, he said, "Tell you what, good man. You run along to your farm, feed your birds and so forth. I'll store these items safely in the supply truck, wait here for the children, and give them a ride back to camp and all that. I imagine they shall return soon enough."

His offer sounded more like a command that Jeepers dare not disobey. Jeepers had no choice but to nod and climb into the Jeep.

Rachel felt a heavy tightness in her chest, and suddenly realized that she had been holding her breath since Nigel first arrived. Heart pounding, arms and legs shivering from the cool breeze blowing across her wet clothes, she exhaled slowly. She looked at Elliot. He returned her glance with a look of defeat that almost hid the sparkle of his green eyes.

Nigel slapped the Jeep fender twice, signaling Jeepers on his way. The turkey farmer sped off, leaving them alone with Mr. British Black Marketeer. He kicked a pile of loose gravel in Selah's direction.

"So . . . where are those two hiding, you stupid animal? They can't have gotten far." A brief stop at the supply truck gave Nigel time to drop their packs and treasures inside the canvas covering above the tailgate. He gathered several items—his hat, some rope, a pistol—and slung a pair of binoculars around his neck.

All this time Rachel had grown colder and colder. Her wet clothes clung to her body like icy mummy wrappings. Her shivers had given way to a constant shaking, and her teeth began to chatter behind her numb lips. She shifted her feet uncomfortably for a better position in the tree, but in doing so her shoes scraped out a loud *crusssskkk!* against the branch bark. Nigel's eagle eye whirled toward the orchard. The binoculars snapped to attention on his face, and he scanned the area, first around the stone fence, then beyond it into the orchard. Rachel huddled against a branch beside her with her eyes closed tightly, hoping the gentle bounce of leaves would hide her.

Finally she opened one eye. The thieving archeologist had cinched the rope over one shoulder and, with pistol drawn, he set out across the orchard away from the supply truck on a beeline for Elliot's tree. He reached it, slowed for one long instant . . . then strode past. Elliot remained motionless.

Rachel couldn't bring herself to breathe or swallow

for fear Nigel might hear. She squeezed herself against the nearest large branch to silence her shaking arms and legs. But her mind cried out in fear, for she knew it was impossible to outwit him.

Halfway across the orchard he halted his hiking search. Slowly, deliberately, he began working his way back toward the truck, stopping at each tree as he went. It was only a matter of time before he found them now. Clearly, he knew they had climbed into hiding. Tree by tree, he stood next to each trunk and surveyed the branches with deadly care. Finding nothing, he moved to the next and to the next and to the next, growing ever closer to Elliot's tree.

Rachel watched in helplessness. This was her fault—she had snooped the journal; she had learned Nigel's dark secret. She could do nothing now but give Nigel what he wanted. But without the journal, they had nothing. Not even a shred of evidence that Nigel was a thief. It would be their word against that of the Archeological Superman whose list of accomplishments was nearly as long as his black market sales list.

Suddenly Nigel spoke.

"I know you're here, the both of you. And I shall find you sooner or later. We might as well make it sooner and be done with it. After all . . . it's the journal I want. Once I have it, we'll all return to the dig together."

If it's all so simple, then what's the gun for? Rachel thought.

He moved to the tree next to Elliot's. "Splendid artifacts you've stumbled onto, by the way—they shall be a fine contribution to the Israel Museum in Jerusalem.

I can arrange for the Museum to list your names along with mine as collectors, if you like." He searched the branches overhead, found nothing, and prepared to move on.

"Stealing a man's journal," he went on. "A terrible thing to do. I doubt very much your Uncle Mason would approve, Rachel, don't you agree?"

Rachel let the journal drop from her fingers. It slapped flat against the ground fifteen meters behind Nigel. Then she lowered her feet to the bottom branch and swooped down from the tree with a jarring *thump!*

He spun to face her, brandishing the gun.

"There's your foolish journal," she said, trembling with cold, fear, and anger.

"Aha!" Nigel's smile became a row of pearly jewels. "So it is! I knew it couldn't have gotten far." He retrieved the journal and cradled the nasty book like a baby in his arms. After a moment of long thought, he shoved the journal into his back pocket. "Now . . . where is that bright cousin of yours?"

"Halfway to Lachish by now, I imagine." Rachel forced a weak smile. "The last time I saw him he had black market business to take care of. Involving you, actually."

His smile remained fixed. "You're not a very good liar."

"Yes, she is," Elliot replied as he dropped from his tree. "Most of the time, that is."

"What are you doing!" hollered Rachel. "He's got his precious journal and he's got me! He doesn't need you!"

"Not true," Nigel said. He motioned with his pistol for Elliot to stand beside Rachel.

"I need you both. I can't very well have you two spreading nasty stories about my work now, can I? All of this black market rot. Really is nothing to it, actually."

"Then give us the journal and take us back to the dig," offered Elliot.

"Oh, I'm afraid I can't do that."

At that moment Rachel noticed that Selah had followed Nigel into the orchard. Like a loyal dog, the goat now stood at his heels and chose that instant to gingerly nip the back of his pants. Startled, he jerked forward as the goat deftly snatched the journal and galloped away—the leather-bound book hanging from its crooked mouth like a candy bar wrapper. Nigel immediately took chase on a path that led deeper into the orchard. Although Selah was small and quick, Nigel's size and motivation would be no match for the pygmy goat. The distraction would last only a moment.

"Come on!" Elliot ran in the opposite direction to scale the low stone wall. Rachel followed until she saw his intended destination—the supply truck.

"Are you insane?" she strained out through a whisper.

"Just get in!" He hopped through the canvas cover and grabbed her shoulders to tug her over the tailgate. But she resisted.

"This is suicide! I will not . . ."

Her feet left the ground as Elliot pulled with all of his might. Awkwardly, she tumbled into the rear bed of the truck with Elliot closing the canvas curtain behind them. When she recovered, she grabbed the collar of his shirt and aimed her fury into his eyes. But before she could speak, a splitting *clap!* rang out beyond the orchard wall—the sound of a single pistol shot.

CHAPTER 14

"Selah!" Rachel gasped. She let go of Elliot's shirt and spun around.

Elliot clamped his hand over her lips so tightly she thought she would suffocate. He held her in a bear hug from behind until she quit squirming and promised with a nod not to say anything. Then he peeled his hand from her mouth.

"Not a word, all right?" Elliot warned her. He spoke in a hushed whisper. "Gather these blankets together in the front corner of the truck bed, now!"

"But . . ." Elliot threw a firm finger in her face. He was serious. Dead serious. She felt her jaw slap shut, and together they yanked the blankets into a baggy pile. Elliot swiftly crawled under the pile, then motioned for her to do the same, which she did. He finished their makeshift stowaway job by pulling blankets over their heads.

Once hidden, they lay in the darkened truck in silence. Rachel, now afraid to say anything, remained still as stone—except for her chattering teeth. One minute went by. Then two. Finally the silence became too much for her.

In a weak whisper she asked, "What's happening? What is he doing?"

"Looking for us, I hope," the pile of blankets beside her whispered back.

She waited another silent minute before asking her real question—the one she dreaded answering herself.

"That was a pistol shot we heard earlier, wasn't it?" Elliot didn't answer. She tried to hide the tremble in her voice as she asked again: "He's shot Selah, hasn't he?"

"We don't know that for sure," Elliot replied in his cool, calm manner. "Selah's a pretty smart goat, if there is such a thing. Who knows? He might have slipped away." He waited just long enough for Rachel to doubt his words, then added: "After all, you thought I was a goner, too, didn't you?"

The distant echo of shoes thudding on wet ground silenced them both.

"Blast them!" The sound of Nigel's boots kicking loose gravel followed. His feet jumped over the stone fence, trotted near the truck, and soon moved from one side of the truck to the other. Rachel could picture him inspecting the horizon with his binoculars, all the while grumbling about their escape. Soon the creaky driver's door opened, then slammed shut as Nigel prepared to drive them away.

"It's working," whispered Elliot. "He thinks we've escaped into the hills."

"One of us nearly did," she answered hoarsely. A picture of Selah running madly up a hillside with Nigel close behind, gun in hand, flashed in her brain. She fought the image by closing her eyes and nestling deeper into the heap of blankets for warmth. What she had done in the orchard—facing Nigel—*seemed* brave and honorable. But she did it only because Nigel would have found her anyway. Selah, on the other hand, was in no danger. He didn't have to steal the journal, nor did he have anything to gain by leading Nigel away so she and Elliot could escape. The goat was the true hero. Selah had more than repaid her for his "rescue" from the railroad track.

The truck engine sparked and whined into first gear. Hidden by the noise of the racing engine, Elliot tossed off his blankets and spoke up again.

"Evidence. That's what we need. We don't have the journal, but we might find something here in Nigel's black market stash."

As the supply truck rocked along the graveled road, he crawled in a clumsy circle, barely able to keep his balance in the swaying truck. Halfway to the tailgate, a dip in the road nearly tumbled him over. He shook his head in frustration. Rachel squirmed from beneath her blankets and tried not to think about the poor little goat. Inside the dark canvas cover it was difficult to see anything. The bumpy ride made it difficult to move around or to rummage through bags without noisily arousing Nigel's suspicions. But she did manage to reach her hiking bag and retrieve Elliot's flashlight. The button clicked under her thumb, sending a narrow beam of light to the rear of the truck. Elliot directed her aim while hurriedly searching each bag. Artifact after artifact appeared in his hands, including several of the inked pots Nigel was supposed to deliver to the Israel Museum. Apparently they were high-profit items on the black market.

"He's got a traveling archeology exhibit in here!" Elliot croaked as he returned to the blanket pile. "All of it stolen."

She shined the flashlight under her own chin to make her point to Elliot and his trusting ways. "And he will have an excuse for each one. Don't you see? Nigel has been at this for quite some time, and he's very good at it. Thievery, I mean." Rachel leaned back against the truck bed frame. In doing so, her fingers struck something hard and cold lying beside her. She rotated the flashlight down to her hand. A metallic glint appeared.

"What is that?" Elliot reached across her, grasped the object, and lifted. It didn't budge. Using both hands, he hefted the long metal point into his lap with a small grunt. Immediately Rachel recognized the artifact. It was the iron blade Elliot had rescued from the pantry while burning breakfast eggs a day earlier. "The spear point!" An odd look crossed his face in the dim light. "This was on Dr. Cunningham's nightstand yesterday. He's got to know it's missing."

"Unless he gave it to Nigel to deliver . . . "

"No!" Elliot interrupted. "I told him I thought it might be the spear point of Goliath. He was so fascinated with the idea that he planned to study it himself."

As his voice trailed into silence, the truck brakes

screeched, and the canvas frame rattled to a clattering halt. Rachel fumbled her blanket back over her head.

"He's heard us, hasn't he!" she panicked.

"Shhh!" Elliot scrambled back to the safety of his blankets, barely breathing. After two long, tense moments, the gears groaned, and the truck jerked forward. For five seconds the wheels ran smoothly. Then a small bump returned them to the usual rollicking ride.

"The highway," Elliot whispered. "That was the main highway we just crossed. Ten more minutes and we pass Aron's farm."

"Jeepers! Of course! He knows all about Nigel!" Rachel felt a surge of hope.

"But you heard Dr. Cunningham yesterday. Many of the local people are suspects in all of this black market business. You and I know Aron is as good as gold. Convincing Dr. Cunningham of that may take some doing. He really takes these stolen artifacts personally. And he's likely to believe Nigel."

"Everyone believes Nigel," Rached sneered. "He probably has some local contacts willing to lie for him. He's such a friendly sort." She felt a twinge of guilt, having fallen for Nigel's charm from the first.

They rode in bumpy silence for a time. The grinding gears moved up and down at Nigel's command. Soon the truck began to wind back and forth in tighter curves. They had reached the edges of the *moshav.* Gobbling turkeys cackled in the distance as the supply truck ambled to a stop.

"Why are we stopping here?" Rachel wondered.

Elliot replied with a silent shrug.

Two voices, muffled by the canvas cover, approached the truck. Both were speaking a foreign language. Rachel recognized it as Hebrew—the same tongue spoken by the dig-site workers. The driver's door opened. Nigel bounced from the truck and replied, first in broken Hebrew, then in clear English with his cheery British accent.

"Take two of the ostraca," he was saying. His voice grew louder as the three neared the tailgate. An arm stretched through the canvas opening to grab two of the inked pots. "Put them with the turkey farmer's belongings in that building over there. This evening before you leave the dig site, one of you must mention to Dr. Cunningham that you have seen ostraca like those at the dig hidden here at the *moshav*. Do you understand?"

Rachel threw back her blanket to exclaim her indignation, but a strong arm pulled her down. Elliot glared and put his finger to his lips.

She pulled the blanket back over her head.

"What has Jeepers done to him?" she said in her quietest whisper. The answer was obvious. Nigel had mastered a first-class scheme: ruining the reputation of the only person, besides them, who could rat on him. Though hesitant to admit it, Rachel knew she and Nigel had a few things in common. Which explained why she hated him so—he mirrored a part of her she didn't particularly like. The men's footsteps trailed away from the the truck.

"Aron's only crime was being there when we needed

him," Elliot observed.

That only made Rachel feel worse. Next to Elliot, Jeepers was the closest friend she had at the moment. And now he would be branded a thief. A terrible thought struck her.

"They won't chop off his hand, will they? The way they tried with Nigel?"

"Goodness Agnes!" Elliot whispered. "What are you talking about?"

"That scar on Nigel's wrist—Jeepers says it is 'the mark of the fortunate thief.'"

Elliot nodded his understanding.

"Aron is no thief. We'll make sure everyone knows that."

The two men soon finished their business, and Nigel retraced a path to the driver's door. Then he called out. "Oh, by the way. Those two children who were here this morning? Seems they have taken a keen interest in our work. Too keen, I'm afraid. They're hiding in the orchards just north of Adullam. Pay them a *visit*, won't you?"

The driver's door clunked shut and the truck jolted forward toward the ruins at Lachish less than two kilometers away. The lump in Rachel's throat felt like a giant grapefruit.

A few minutes later, the truck made its final stop—at the dig site. Elliot turned back the edge of his blanket for a final survey of the truck bed.

"We've got to stop Nigel before he hides these artifacts away forever."

"No, wait!" Rachel schemed. "Let's hear what he tells Uncle Mason and Dr. Cunningham. How is he going to explain our disappearance? That blasted journal of his, lost or found, will still be his undoing. He's got to lie to cover himself. And once he does, our side of the story will sound much more believable."

For the first time since leaving the orchard, Elliot cracked a faint smile. "So . . . let him hang himself with his own words, right?"

"Believe me, it's worked on me many times," Rachel confessed. Elliot's smile grew slightly. "Well, once, per- haps," she quickly added.

The driver's door of the supply truck swung shut. On cue, Rachel and Elliot scurried beneath the military blankets tossed loosely about the truck bed. The sound of the canvas cover drawing open alerted them that the only thing between them and Nigel was a thin layer of blanket and three meters of empty space. Rachel could hear him breathing. The truck bed bounced under his weight as he mounted the tailgate and stowed the artifacts—*their* artifacts—into his museum bags.

"Nigel, old boy! You're back a bit early. Got all of the ostraca delivered, I take it?" The voice belonged to Dr. Cunningham.

"Uh . . . yes, quite." Zipping bags told Rachel he had managed to hide almost everything. A giant's spear might be somewhat more difficult, however. She peeked from beneath the blanket just long enough to see Nigel throw a covering over the wooden artifact. "Is the tea on?" he asked.

"You are just in time!" Rachel heard a friendly slap on the back, followed by the crunching of two pairs of hiking boots fading toward the mess hall. "How was the drive to Jerusalem?"

"It went well. Although I had an odd experience this morning at the *moshav*. When I dropped the children there, the turkey farmer certainly had a lot of questions about our dig—how successful have we been, what types of artifacts, and whatnot. Might just be small talk I suppose, but . . . one can never be too sure . . . "

"Mmmm," came Dr. Cunningham's thoughtful voice. "You know . . . that spear point Mason's son found yesterday? It's missing from my nightstand."

"Really?" Nigel's reply sounded full of surprise. "By the way, are the children back yet?"

"Why, no."

"Oh." Nigel gave a studied pause. "Well, if this turkey farmer is caught up in the black market trade of selling artifacts, there's no telling what he might promise the children for their silence . . . or what he might do to secure it." The mess hall door swung shut.

Rachel jumped to her feet.

"I don't believe it. He's ruined Jeepers' good name, he's trying to have us killed, yet he acts as though he's concerned about our welfare. He's thought of everything!"

"Not quite," Elliot assured her. "Dad will believe us. But without that journal, we still have no hard proof. Just the opinion of two twelve-year-old kids."

"I'm nearly thirteen, and so are you. And we can both

drive a Jeep . . . sort of. That should count for something."

They sat silently in the truck for quite some time, Elliot thinking and Rachel fuming—and wishing she were inside sipping hot tea. At last Elliot spoke up.

"Okay. We need to move these artifacts before Nigel comes back. And we probably should find you some dry clothes."

"Oh, right. Let's make sure these old ostriches and that ugly gold pot of yours are safe, *then* we shall worry about whether Rachel has fatal frostbite," she growled.

"*Ostraca*. Now, hop out of the tailgate. I'll hand Nigel's bags down, and you set them alongside the truck. But do it quietly."

Rachel swung her damp pant legs over the tailgate, through the slit in the canvas covering.

"What do you intend to do with them?"

"I'm not sure. Probably stow them under our bunks for now, until we think of something. Nigel doesn't dare ask where they are, or he'll give himself away."

He handed three bulging bags into her waiting arms, then slid out the wooden spear shaft. The iron blade came last. Elliot held it against his chest and carried it over the tailgate. But no sooner had they gathered the collection into one neat pile than the mess door creaked open, and Dr. Nigel Chatsworth emerged.

CHAPTER 15

"Let me unload a few things from the truck," Nigel was saying to Dr. Cunningham. "I'll be back in a flash to take a few measurements at the east gate."

Uncle Mason followed close behind them, his field pack slung over his shoulder.

"Hi, Dad."

"Well! Elliot, Rachel!" His bear-hug arms opened to them. "We were worried about you!" He wrapped an arm around each of them. "Did you run into problems?"

"No, not at all," piped Rachel, although her wet clothes indicated otherwise.

Nigel's smug expression melted to one of disbelief.

"It's been an interesting day, actually," she went on. "Hello, Nigel. Pleasure to see you again so soon. I trust you are well . . . we certainly are." She turned to Elliot. "He looks as if he has seen a ghost, don't you agree?" She gave the black marketeer a big wave and flashed her most irritating smile.

"Any luck hunting artifacts?" Uncle Mason asked.

"Oh . . . you wouldn't believe what we've *uncovered*."

"Really?" chimed in Dr. Cunningham. He chuckled. "Well, out with it then!"

Like the snake that he was, Nigel struck first.

"I'm curious . . . how did you two slip back into camp?" He turned to his two colleagues. "I am concerned about their friend, the turkey farmer. He may still be lurking about."

"Yes, we must warn you about that farmer," Dr. Cunningham began. "We think he is to blame for some disappearing artifacts."

Before she could answer their unfair accusations, the familiar sound of a sputttering Jeep engine reached Rachel's ears. *Jeepers!* He could not have picked a worse time to pay them a visit. There was no telling what lies Nigel had told about him over tea. Rachel tried waving him away, but he simply waved grandly in return.

Nigel practically growled his suspicions. "There . . . she's trying to warn him about something. I fear this black market rot is just as I suspected. He has managed to win over these silly children, with bribery no doubt." The Jeep passed the barracks and slowed as it approached them. Nigel called to several nearby dig workers. "Don't let this man leave camp, do you understand?" His eyes fell to the pile of artifacts at their feet. "He's returned for these priceless items. And he has used the children to acquire them."

The Jeep bounced to a stop beneath Jeepers' gold-toothed smile. Rachel noticed how the Jeep's long, afternoon shadow fell directly across Nigel, as if separating him from everyone else.

"Good afternoon, doctors. I am Aron Segal. I believe I've found something of yours that was lost." Jeepers held up a leather-bound book with a gold latch. He handed it directly to Uncle Mason, who seemed a bit confused.

"Yes!" Rachel squealed. "Yes, yes!"

Elliot adjusted his glasses and placed his hand on her shoulder with a broad smile.

Nigel wormed his way past them to reach Jeepers.

"You seem to have found my journal," he began. "What an odd coincidence. It went missing at the same time several ostraca disappeared this morning. At your farm, in fact." He reached out to take the book from Uncle Mason, but Rachel dived between the two men and snatched it away.

"Goodness Agnes, Rachel! What are you doing?" came Uncle Mason's shocked reply.

Before she could explain herself, a dig worker stepped into the circle of people grouped at the stone walls. He bowed his head humbly.

"I must confess. I have seen ostraca hidden at this man's farm. And I have seen him trade other artifacts for money."

"Why hadn't you spoken up before now?" Dr. Cunningham jumped in.

Nigel grabbed at the book. "There, you see? I suspected this."

"Wait, wait." Uncle Mason raised his stocky arms above the fray. "Everyone take a deep breath. We'll get to the bottom of this, calmly and properly. Now . . ."

He looked at Rachel, "please give Dr. Chatsworth his journal."

"But Nigel, er . . . Dr. Chatsworth *is* the bottom of this. He is a fortunate thief who sells stolen Flintstone pots with big ears and he tried to steal the Giant Goldfish spear from us just after Elliot drowned in the cistern. And *then* he shot my goat!"

The small, nimble frame of Dr. Ian Cunningham moved to the middle of the tight circle they had formed around Nigel and Rachel. He lifted a polite finger to Rachel.

"I know you've just said something terribly important, but for the life of me, I have no idea what it is. Dr. Conner is correct. We all need an explanation. Would someone care to give one, please? Nigel?"

Nigel stood shifting his weight from one foot to the other. He looked quite uncomfortable. But, bright man that he was, he had a quick answer.

"I, too, have attempted to get to the bottom of all this. Stolen artifacts, secret meetings . . . I've documented all I could learn about these distasteful activities in hopes of stopping them once and for all. It's all there," he said, motioning to Rachel's hands, "in my journal."

Rachel felt as if she had received a stinging slap across her face. Nigel had just passed off his entire journal as a record of honor.

Elliot stepped before them with his back to the stone walls.

"Nigel is right. Everything is there in his journal, just as he says it is. Everything."

"What are you saying!" Rachel screeched.

"Take a look, Dad," Elliot went on. He took the book from Rachel and passed it on. "Start with the July 11 entry, when he stole a scribe statue and a gold necklace from the Egyptian Museum in Cairo."

"What? I remember when those pieces were stolen. It caused quite an uproar among the museum curators." Dr. Cunningham lifted the leather book from Uncle Mason's hands and turned to July. His brow curled down over his eyes as he read.

"Now look at September 28. A pair of matching bronze daggers uncovered in Palestine—sold to a buyer in Europe for a mere $245,000."

Both Uncle Mason and Dr. Cunningham were reading now. They flipped forward to October's table of black market sales.

"That table," explained Elliot, "lists all of Nigel's major sales this summer—weapons, statues, jewelry— all stolen."

"This is preposterous!" Nigel huffed.

"Is it?" Rachel challenged. "Then perhaps you can explain these bags of artifacts you've stashed away in the supply truck—including the inked pots you were supposed to deliver to the museum."

Nigel answered her calmly.

"I decided to tidy them up a bit before dropping them off. So I've brought them back for a good cleaning."

"I suppose you intended to clean this as well?" Rachel nearly tumbled forward lifting the heavy metal spear point from their artifact pile.

"The spear point." Dr. Cunningham's gaze moved from the iron weapon to Nigel Chatsworth. "Five minutes ago you accused this farmer of stealing these items, yet you have had them all along."

"Now, see here!" Nigel said. "You're going on as if I were a common thief!"

Uncle Mason read a little further in the journal. A look of surprise suddenly crossed his face. He glanced up from the pages. "Twit?" he read aloud.

"Oh, never mind that 'twit' garbage!" snapped Rachel. "What does it say he planned to do with the spear point?"

She knew she had asked the right question by the way Nigel swallowed—slow and hard. The two older archeologists read silently, then looked at one another. Dr. Cunningham spoke.

"So . . . it seems you had found yourself an Iraqi buyer for the complete spear of Goliath. Imagine his surprise had you tried to peddle him nothing more than this iron spear point." Dr. Cunningham slapped the journal shut. "Apparently, stealing from the archeological community was no challenge. Next you intended to double-cross a black market buyer. You are braver than I realized, Nigel. And much more foolish." His tone took on that of a father correcting a young child. "I don't know what to say. . . . I am so very disappointed in you."

Nigel said nothing. He simply stared at the ground—his brash manner and witty conversation had evaporated in disgrace. In the end, he really was just a common thief.

"Uh . . . this may not be the best time to mention this," Elliot broke in after a long silence. "But the spear point . . . it's genuine. The real thing."

"How do you know?" asked Uncle Mason. Elliot rarely made statements he couldn't back with facts, and Uncle Mason wanted the facts.

"Because we found the rest of it. When I was trapped in the cistern, I—"

"When you were *what*?" crowed Uncle Mason.

"Long story, Dad. You always say a picture is worth a thousand words, right? Well, take a look at this." He drew the carved, wooden spear shaft from the artifact pile.

Uncle Mason's smartly-trimmed beard parted enough for his jaw to drop open. His lips pushed forward into what Rachel expected to be the mother of all "Goodness Agneses." But Dr. Cunningham beat him to the punch.

"Goodness Gladys!" he exclaimed in his distinctive British accent. "Mason . . . do you really suppose it could be the actual spear of Goliath of Gath?"

"It matches everything I've read about it. And with that iron tip—"

"The spear point fits the shaft perfectly. I tried it out already," Elliot explained.

The three of them hovered over the weapon like old geese pecking at a pile of grain. Rachel heard nothing but "ooohs" and "ahhhs" and words like Philistines and Tangerines. In the midst of it all, Elliot told them the story of the cistern and the water and explained all about Selah's daring deeds and Jeepers' help—and, saving the best for last, he related how Rachel risked a Jeep trip to save his life.

"I'm the one who found the stick, you know," she called out at the appropriate point in his story.

"We've got some serious research to do on this thing," said Uncle Mason.

"We do indeed." Dr. Cunningham fumbled in his vest pocket for a magnifying lens. As he began his inch-by-inch examination of the spear's carvings, Uncle Mason approached Jeepers' Jeep.

"I'm very sorry about all this, Mr. Segal," Uncle Mason began. "I know you didn't come here to be called a liar and a thief." They shook hands. "Thanks for returning the journal. We'll turn it over to the authorities along with the stolen artifacts."

"You really should be thanking the goat," Jeepers replied. "It was Selah who retrieved the journal. I am simply the messenger delivering it."

"I wish we *could* thank Selah," sighed Rachel sadly. "Already I miss his candy-bar breath. Poor little goat. Where on earth did you find the journal?"

Jeeper's face brightened.

"I found it here . . ." He reached over the Jeep's driver's seat to the rear floorboard. Then with a grunt he raised himself up. A large, damp mass of matted hair filled his arms. Four skinny legs dangled below Elliot's lost hat, perched atop a pair of flattened goat ears.

Bleeaahhh!

"My goat!" Rachel scrambled to the Jeep and filled her arms with the wet animal.

"And my hat!" rejoiced Elliot. He placed it on his own head while tousling the goat's ears. "See . . . I told you this was my lucky hat!"

After a long hug, Rachel turned the pygmy goat loose to frolic among the ancient walls behind them. Suddenly she noticed a strange odor.

"What *is* that *smell*?" She felt her face twist into a sour expression.

Elliot leaned against the Jeep, adjusted his glasses, and crossed his arms below a smile.

"It *was* Selah," he cheerfully pointed out. "Now it's *you*."

CHAPTER 16

EPILOGUE

"Any word yet . . . about Nigel?" asked Elliot.

Dr. Cunningham leaned forward for a second portion of bread.

"Yes, actually. Dr. Ramsay from the Israel Museum called a short time ago. Seems Nigel was taken into official custody yesterday in Jerusalem, as were two local workers. Formal charges and all that sort of thing will be forthcoming, I imagine. That journal of his has allowed the museum to track down several stolen artifacts already." The good doctor shook his head. "Nigel always was one to keep careful notes. His clean record up to this point should work in his favor, but he won't be visiting any digs or museums for a long, long time." He shook his head again in sincere disappointment. "Such a bright young man, too. With a bright future. Tragic . . . simply tragic."

"Apparently his gift for understanding the past just wasn't enough for him," observed Uncle Mason. "He became too caught up in the greed for his own future."

The wiry old archeologist nodded in agreement. He tore his bread portion in two, then held up the pieces, one in each hand.

"Well then, in any event, if it weren't for our little delay here at Lachish, I would not have had the pleasure of celebrating this American Thanksgiving of yours!"

"Such as it is!" laughed Uncle Mason. "You do realize, Ian, that bread and fruit are Thanksgiving Day appetizers back in the States—not the whole meal!" He drew his sturdy hand across their mess hall table, where two loaves of local bread and a bowl of store-bought fruit dotted the bare tabletop.

"Yes, yes, quite. I've celebrated a few Thanksgivings myself. Quite the feast, what with the big roasted bird and all that."

"And the oyster dressing," Rachel chimed in. "You know," she went on with her nose held high in the air, "it isn't necessarily an American holiday. The pilgrims were British, after all."

"Well . . . there you are," Dr. Cunningham added. "No wonder it is such a splendid holiday!"

The hum of an engine outside the mess hall brought Elliot to his feet. He peered through the window.

"It's Aron."

"Really?" Uncle Mason stood. "I'm surprised he would bother coming here after all of Nigel's accusations."

Bleeaahhh!

"And Selah's with him," added Elliot, smiling.

The four of them went out to greet the turkey farmer. And the goat, of course. Just as he had done days earlier, Jeepers reached into the weathered backseat of his rusting Jeep. But this time, instead of producing a goat, he lifted a freshly-plucked turkey, ready for roasting. The plump, bald bird twirled slowly below his raised fist. Jeepers' gold tooth shone beneath his bushy mustache.

"This is for you. To help you give thanks on this, your Holy Day."

"Goodness Agnes! What a bird!" boomed Uncle Mason. "I hope you plan to stay and help us eat it."

Jeepers smiled. Then, with a twinkle in his eye matching his gold tooth, he pointed over his shoulder. Two more vehicles—another worn Jeep and an old sideboard truck—were winding up the road from the *moshav.*

"My family will help cook," he grinned. "*And* eat."

The jingle of the dig site telephone called Uncle Mason back inside the mess hall. He was chatting with someone over the speakerphone when everyone, including both loads of Jeepers' family and the goat, huddled into the kitchen. Rachel knew right away that it must be Uncle Mason's secretary, Arlene.

"Oh, no, no," he was saying. "No problem at all. The students can use the SIMA workroom if they like. No rush. We won't be home until Saturday."

"Fine, I'll let them know," the spry voice answered. "Is Rachel there?"

"Right here, Arlene," Rachel piped up. Talks with Arlene always managed to cheer her, even over the telephone. The eagle-eyed secretary had a special understanding of Rachel. Somehow she always knew just what to say or do to make Rachel feel important. No matter that Arlene looked very much like a silver-headed bird of some sort.

"Happy Thanksgiving, dearie. You've received several pieces of mail recently. I believe one is from your relatives in England. I'll have all of your letters here for you when you arrive."

"Thanks, Arlene."

"Oh, by the way," Arlene's voice crackled over the speakerphone. "Your mother called . . . "

"And?" Rachel suddenly realized that she had crossed her arms as if to protect against whatever it was her mother had to say.

"She wants to buy you a nice holiday dress and wondered what color you prefer."

She glanced first at Uncle Mason—leaning over the makeshift kitchen table in his dig-site khaki clothes—then at Dr. Cunningham, who was dressed just like him. Next her eyes fell on Elliot, who casually shrugged his shoulders and tugged at the brim of his moth-eaten hat. Finally she reached out and dragged her fingers through Selah's matted coat.

"Tell her I'd like a goat-hair dress," Rachel answered thoughtfully. "Preferably one with a matching hat. And make it all . . . khaki." Jeepers threw her a big smile. "Oh, Arlene?" she added with her eyes focused on Jeepers' tooth. "I'd nearly forgotten. Tell her it simply must have gold buttons."

A long silence hung over the speakerphone. At last

Arlene responded.

"Whatever you say, dearie." Another long pause. Then, "Your uncle tells me we need to make space in the central display room here at the SIMA museum for a spear of some sort—one you and Elliot discovered."

"Yes." She made sure Elliot was listening. "The Israel Museum is letting us borrow it for a time. We shall display it in the special 'Rachel Ashton' room. Please see that a new display case is prepared, if you would." Elliot just rolled his eyes, but Dr. Cunningham wiggled his eyebrows in approval—which, to Rachel's delight, seemed to make Elliot a bit jealous.

Uncle Mason collected his remaining messages from Arlene, while Jeepers' family set straight to work clanging available pots and pans and searching for something big enough to hold the plucked turkey. Dr. Cunningham filled five porcelain mess hall cups with his special tea blend.

"I've been saving this for the proper occasion," he announced. "And I do believe this is it. Shall we have a toast, then?" He offered his tea cup over the wooden table's center. "To good health and happiness. And to future expeditions . . . may they all go well." He nodded toward the massive spear shaft of Goliath, now reunited with its long-lost spear point.

"Elliot! I just remembered . . . " interrupted Rachel. "Do we have more to celebrate? You never did tell us what you found inside that horrid-looking gold pot!"

"Oh, nothing much." He hid a grin. "Just these." Four smooth stones emerged from his vest pocket with a tug. He rattled them with his fingers. "*Wadi* stones, from the valley of the giant. I'm betting the original set had five stones. The fifth one felled a giant. Now . . . if we could only find the sling that threw it. . . . "

Rachel cleared her throat to silence him and raised her full cup of tea.

"To Selah, the snooping goat. And to Jeepers . . . for everything." Elliot's cup rose to meet her own.

Then Aron Segal raised his cup.

"To turkeys," he declared over the clatter of kitchen cookware. "Especially roasted ones." Then he looked across the table at Rachel, his gold tooth reflecting the afternoon sunlight. "But I am curious—these 'Jeepers' you talk about. What are they?"

Elliot looked at Rachel over his wire-rimmed glasses, clearly waiting for her answer.

"Oh, it's a long story, actually," she weaseled. Reaching across the table, she clinked her cup against the one in Jeepers' hand. "Let's just say they go well . . . with turkey."

THE END

The TRUTH of the QUEST

This story is entirely fictional. The spear of Goliath has not been found. But the Bible states that David won the giant's weapons in battle, and later, before becoming king of Judah, he regained Goliath's spear from a Hebrew priest. David lived among the Philistines for a time and then went to the caves of Adullam, which are located in the hill country of modern-day Israel. You can read more about David and Israel, old and new, in these books:

Archaeology of the Bible. Magnus Magnusson.
New York: Simon and Shuster, 1977, 239 pages.

Bible Lands (Eyewitness Books). Jonathan N. Tubb.
New York: Alfred A. Knopf, 1991, 63 pages.

A Guide to the Archaeological Sites of Israel, Egypt and North Africa. Courtlandt Canby, with Arcadia Kocybala. New York: Facts on File, 1990, 278 pages.

The Holy Bible, I & II Samuel, and I Chronicles.